MW01611335

38 Chestnuts

A Korean American Novel

Mary J Park

Hot Pot
Publishing

38 CHESTNUTS : A Korean American Novel
Copyright © 2014 by MARY J PARK.

This book is a work of fiction. Names, characters, businesses, organizations, places, events and incidents either are the product of the author's imagination or are used fictitiously. Any resemblance to actual persons, living or dead, events, or locales is entirely coincidental.

For information contact: www.hotpotpublishing.com

Author photo: Toshikophoto

ISBN: 978-0-9672495-4-4

First Edition: November 2014

10 9 8 7 6 5 4 3 2 1

Dedicated to my parents

Table of Contents

38 Chestnuts

A Korean American Novel

History, despite its wrenching pain,
Cannot be unlived, and if faced
With courage, need not be lived again

Maya Angelou
On the Pulse of Morning
Inaugural Poem
January 20, 1993

Chapter One
UMA

A S UMA WATCHED HER DAUGHTER, Sunny, walk down the aisle on her father's arm, she fully grasped the old Korean proverb, "a married daughter is no better than a stranger." She could only hope that Sunny would not commit any of the seven evils of women: disobeying her in-laws, bearing no son, sexual looseness, being jealous, carrying a hereditary disease, talking too much, and stealing. Even a false rumor could result in irrevocable dishonor and shame to the entire family.

A woman followed the three men in her life: her father upon birth, her husband upon marriage, and her eldest son upon the death of her husband. The last third was to make up for the suffering endured by the first two. At last, she could boss around her daughter-in-law and have the complete adoration and respect of her son. She would be served like a queen and wouldn't have to lift a finger. Her only responsibilities were to supervise and criticize her daughter-in-law's cooking, cleaning, and raising of her grandchildren.

There was no one to take care of Uma in her old age and there was no one to blame, but herself. She didn't have a safety son.

THE LAST TIME UMA saw her son was in the fall of 1950. They were home, in Hamhung, North Korea. Home, where wild geese flew under misty mountaintops and red maple leaves danced through the air. Home, where muddy rivers turned to streams and flowed into rice fields. Home, where harvested rice stalks sunned themselves in the cool breeze as eager farmers brought their goods to market on ox-drawn carts. Weary mothers carried heavy loads of cabbage and radish on their heads with wailing babies tied to their backs. Shop owners lifted creaking metal doors. Villagers pushed each other through the hustle and bustle and jostled for the last pear. The smell of crispy *bindaetteok*, mung bean pancakes fried in grease, wafted through the air as soldiers with red armbands stood on the corner of a worn down police station with torn signs in Japanese. A communist flag waved in shifting winds as the Supreme Leader Kim Il Sung's bloated face, plastered to the side of the station, followed your every move.

38 Chestnuts

A tofu vendor carried a wooden box on his shoulder and strolled down the street rhythmically ringing his bell. "Get your tofu! Get your fresh tofu."

Uma couldn't recall the last time anyone had called her by her given name. Ever since her first child was born, she was *Uma*, mom, to everyone. Her plump lips, that she tried to suck in until only a thin sliver showed, overshadowed her narrow face, lined beyond her thirty-five years. She wrapped a white scarf around her head and jumped into her *gomusin* to catch the tofu vendor. The back of her heels flattened her rubber canoe-shaped shoes as she dragged her feet across the courtyard, deepening grooves on familiar tracks.

Inside the house, Apa limped to a bureau. The responsibilities of *sunsengnim*, teacher, and *Apa*, dad, lay heavily on his stooped shoulders. His hair turned grey overnight when he reached forty. He was only a shadow of the man Uma had married. He lit a stick of incense and fanned it. The glowing embers smoldered releasing faint smoke signals. He longingly gazed at a picture frame.

Uma almost forgot that this was a special day. She could only afford one hard-boiled egg, but she made sure to make *miyokkuk*. She soaked the kelp overnight. The slimy seaweed slithered through her icy fingers as she rinsed it several times to make sure that no sand remained. She ate so much seaweed soup after giving birth, the fishy smell made her nauseated. But tradition dictated that you must have *miyokkuk* on your birthday. *I'll be glad when I complete five cycles of the twelve lunar animals and turn sixty years old. Then, I won't have to eat another bowl of miyokkuk,* she thought.

When Apa saw his daughter, Sunny, carrying in a steaming pot of seaweed soup, his mood shifted. Early that morning, Sunny rebraided her hair three times until it laid perfectly down her straight back in a pleasing manner to others. On a canvas of flawless skin, her deep chestnut eyes were offset by the delicate arch of her sparse eyebrows.

Apa lowered himself onto the square cushion at the head of the black lacquer table. Uma placed a pot of rice next to her and sat across from him, second in command. The girls took their seats.

Apa placed the boiled egg in a glazed celadon ceramic holder in front of Sunny. She bowed her head in gratitude, lowered her inquisitive eyes and soaked up her father's attention. Just then, the rice paper door flew open and the son barged into the room. Apa's flow of affection switched off in an instant. He stood up but could not meet his son's eyes for Youngho had become a man who stood a head taller than his father.

"Youngho, what do you think you're doing?" Apa demanded.

Uma's heart pounded at the sight of her beloved son. She leaped up, grabbed his arm, and clutched it against her chest.

"He hasn't had a decent meal in weeks," she pleaded. Apa shot his wife a look that silenced her.

"Get back in the vegetable storage hole!" Apa pointed to the door and lowered himself down next to Sunny.

"Apa, please, can *Oppa,* stay?" Sunny begged. Uma sighed with relief knowing that Apa could not deny his doting daughter.

"All right, but your older brother better be quick," Apa urged.

Uma nodded to Sunny who instinctively got up and sat next to her baby sister, Nabi, on the other side of the table. Uma patted the cushion next to her and Youngho accepted.

Nabi, Uma's final, failed attempt for a safety son, flicked back her two messy braids with her metal chopsticks held in clumsy six-year-old hands.

"What stinks?" Nabi said as she pinched her nose.

"Oh, you don't like the smell of wet burlap bags?" Youngho said. "Then how about a big hug?" He lunged towards Nabi who screamed with delight. Uma slowly nudged the egg in front of Youngho. He, in turn, moved it back in front of Sunny. After the third time, Uma picked up the egg and placed it in front of Youngho.

"He needs his nutrition," Uma declared.

Sunny turned to her father for help, but he did not see her. His gaze was fixed on the door as the creases on his forehead deepened.

"Umm, rice never tasted so good," exclaimed Youngho as he shoveled another mouthful in.

"Eat, eat more," Uma encouraged, giving him another scoop.

"You better go back," Apa said.

"Just let him finish, please," Uma begged. Apa put down his chopsticks, poured his water into his rice bowl, swirled three times and drank. He turned to Sunny and patted her hand.

"Happy Birthday, Sunny," he said hiding something behind his back. Uma felt helpless; she hated when he did this. As her husband continued, she shook her head with a loud sigh and declared momentary defeat.

He handed Sunny an object wrapped in red cloth embroidered with swans.

"Only yesterday you were just a baby, but now you have grown up to be a young lady."

"Apa, I'm only fifteen," Sunny said blushing.

"Your mother was only a year older than you when we got married." Sunny covered her bashful smile with her hand and unwrapped the cloth that held a hand carved bamboo brush.

"It's made of tiger hair. It belonged to my grandfather, a famous scholar and painter," he said.

She carefully stroked the bristles.

"You're our bright hope . . . for a college graduate," he said. Sunny pondered the gravity of her father's expectations. Youngho turned away and covered his face with his hand to shield his father's disappointment.

Sunny tentatively handed the brush back to her father. Uma ripped the brush out of Sunny's hand, rewrapped it and nodded at Youngho. Sunny stared at her empty hand. Uma believed it was dangerous for girls to have dreams.

"Youngho, go back right now, you *babo*!" Apa exploded. "You have no idea what they're capable of." Youngho was no dummy. Humiliation spread across his beet red cheeks. He opened his mouth for a comeback but clenched his teeth instead. Uma shook her head, begging her son to calm down. Youngho glared at his father. When Uma held the face of her only son in her hands, she felt his hot temples throb. For his mother, Youngho swallowed his father's disrespect for the last time and stormed out. Apa picked up the brush and placed it in Sunny's hands.

THAT NIGHT THEY CAME.

Sunny enveloped her little sister's hand in hers and skillfully guided her ink stone dipped brush across thirsty rice paper. Bursting with eagerness, Nabi tried to shake her sister's hand off hers.

"I can do it by myself," she insisted.

"Open up! Open up! We know he's in there!" Loud pounding against the metal front gate disrupted the brief moment of childhood innocence.

"Stay inside," Apa warned. He carefully rose, put on his overcoat and closed the door behind him. He limped across the courtyard and unlatched the rusty lock.

Two teenaged Communist soldiers with red armbands scowled "Where are you hiding him?"

"Why, good evening, sirs, what can I do for you?" Apa asked as he bowed.

"Where is he?" the baby-faced soldier demanded.

"Who?" Apa asked.

"Don't be stubborn, old man," the lanky soldier warned as he pushed Apa aside and barged into the house.

Uma and the girls stood and bowed to the soldiers with their gaze lowered.

"Where is Youngho?" they asked Uma.

"You're out on such a chilly night, how about a cup of barley tea?"

"We received a report that he had been spotted today."

Uma poured tea into two ceramic cups and placed them on a round serving dish. She raised the dish towards the soldiers.

"Youngho is visiting my brother in the countryside, he's not here," Uma assured them.

The lanky soldier took a sip of tea and spat it out in Uma's face.

"Stop wasting my time, woman."

The soldiers trampled on the girls' painting, ripping it in two. The baby-faced soldier shoved his rifle in Sunny's face, the cold barrel branded her scorching cheek.

"Chung, is that you?" she asked.

"Where is your brother? He must enlist in the Communist army," Chung demanded.

"It's me, Sunny, we were in Teacher Yu's class last year."

"Shut up and tell me where he is."

"We already told you," Apa said. His attempt at diplomacy turned into an order. "Put down the rifle."

Chung pointed the rifle at Apa and forced him to kneel. Boy soldiers at play. The lanky soldier kicked Apa in the ribs and passed him to his comrade.

"Chung, stop!" Sunny screamed.

Chung paused, gave her a smile, and then made the final goal leaving bloody tread marks on Apa's face.

The search continued outside. Uma held her sobbing baby daughter knowing it was too late to shield her from sorrow. Sunny knelt down and cradled Apa's head in her arms.

The soldiers captured Youngho climbing over the crumbling stone wall. They grabbed him by his arms and hauled him into the courtyard. Uma darted out and hung onto Youngho's leg as the soldiers dragged her across the mud.

"You can't take him. He's my only son. Please, I beg you," she pleaded. Chung clubbed her in the face with the butt of his rifle.

"We all must serve the Supreme Leader, Kim Il Sung," Chung declared. "No exceptions." The soldiers tightened their grip on Youngho.

"Uma! Uma!" Youngho screamed as he twisted and kicked, trying to get away.

"Youngho..." Uma leaped towards him, landing face down in the mud.

Her son was gone.

Sunny and Nabi lifted their mother's arms and sat her up like a rag doll. Her legs opened in a 'V', surrendering to the cruelty of life. Her daughters clung to her arms, but Uma shooed them away, beating her fists on the earth. Her dress caked with mud and blood, she shook her fists and shrieked at the sky, "Haven't you already taken enough? What's the use … when you can't protect them? *Aigo*, Youngho, my son, my precious son." A knot clenched her insides that never let go.

UMA PICKED UP THE picture frame from the bureau. She caressed the picture of Jinny, her first born, a natural beauty. Even at the tender age of twelve, her wide forehead, *sangapul*, double eyelids and high nose bridge turned heads. She was destined for a prosperous marriage. When she was just a baby, the neighbors lined up to catch a glimpse of her. They couldn't believe that Uma had given birth to such a beautiful baby. Jinny loved being in the spotlight. She howled if her mother talked to a visitor instead of paying attention to her. Only when the focus was on her, did she slumber. She did not like competition, especially from a boy. In front of adults, she acted like a doting *nuna*, older sister, but when she thought no one was watching, she bit her baby brother Youngho's ears, leaving purple teeth marks.

UP UNTIL FIVE YEARS ago, Uma had lived under Japanese occupation. In 1945, on the brink of losing the war, Japan became even more desperate.

She had sent Jinny to market to buy stalks of *paa*, scallions for the *mukuk*, radish soup. She sliced the white daikon in one-inch squares, sautéed the garlic in sesame oil, added soy sauce, onion, salt and a little bit of beef broth. After she added the meat, she waited until the radish became translucent before she poured in the rest of the broth. After it simmered for a few minutes, she seasoned with black pepper, sesame seeds, and red pepper powder. The only thing missing was the scallions that must go in last so they don't overcook and become mushy.

Dinnertime arrived and her eldest had not returned home. *She's probably yapping away with her friends at the market. Everywhere she goes, she gathers a crowd of admirers who simply want to be in her presence,* Uma thought. She liked to think that she had a hand in Jinny's popularity.

There were no scallions in the *mukuk* that night.

When Apa found out that his wife had sent their daughter out to the market alone, his eyes grew wide and he hollered, "A girl should not be out alone especially in these times."

"It was early afternoon when she left," Uma mumbled.

Apa grabbed his overcoat and hobbled outside. Her husband's alarm triggered her constant sense of dread that lay just beneath the surface. Ever since she became a mother, she couldn't help worrying that something bad was going to happen to her babies. As their mother, she was responsible for keeping them safe.

Uma and Apa searched for Jinny day and night. The vendors at the market, her teachers, her friends, neighbors, no one had seen her, including the scallion vendor. The Japanese police couldn't be bothered with taking a missing person report, especially of a missing Korean girl.

When the tofu vendor whispered in Uma's ear what he had witnessed a week earlier, she crumbled to the ground. He saw Jinny forced into a military truck with a dozen whimpering girls.

ALL HER LIFE, UMA had lived in a Korea that was under occupation by another country. The supposed 'liberators' faces kept changing: Japanese, Russians, Communists, Americans. To Uma, they were all the same, plucking her babies away.

In December of 1950, American fighter jets bombed Hamhung day and night. Uma's next-door neighbor's house was hit and the embers from the explosion shot over into their courtyard. She had Sunny and Nabi put on layers of their warmest clothing. Her daughters helped her pack dried beans and *nurungi*, roasted rice cakes made from leftover rice stuck to the bottom of the pot. When her husband thankfully returned from his latest interrogation by the Communist soldiers, they both knew it was time to leave.

Apa rushed his family outside. Artillery fire rained down on the clay roof. Sunny tried to run back into the house; Apa blocked her. There was no turning back.

THE VILLAGERS CARRIED EVERYTHING they could on their heads, backs, and in ox-drawn carts. Bombed buildings and their victims lined the streets. Apa and Nabi snaked through the chaos. Uma and Sunny followed behind. A naked toddler wailed next to his dead mother. He ran to Uma and grabbed her skirt with his bloody hands. She stroked his tear-streaked face. His anguish slowed to short gulps of hope. Even in the sea of despair, Uma's priorities were clear. She tore each of his tiny fingers from her skirt then hurried away, leaving the boy to fend for himself. Stunned, he stared at his empty palm. Gradually, his fingers curled into a fist.

Uma grabbed Sunny's hand and ran across the burning rice fields as the fighter jets carpet-bombed the field. Apa motioned them into a rice storage container. The four of them sat crouched down with their heads bowed. Nabi covered her ears, her elbows on her knees. The bombs did not rest. A stream of urine formed a puddle under Nabi. Sunny covered her nose and held her breath, but soon she had no choice but to inhale. The girls ate the last of the dried rice and beans. There was no room for Apa to stretch his legs. Entangled, the family fell asleep until silence woke them.

Apa cautiously opened the latch and peeked out. The rice fields were littered with dead soldiers and civilians. Clouds of smoke rose from the village in the distance. Moans and cries filled the empty spaces.

Apa and Nabi forged ahead. Sunny stopped and vomited. Uma bent down and turned over bodies of soldiers in green Communist uniforms with blown off faces and strewn about limbs. She started screaming her son's name, "Youngho, Youngho." Sunny joined her. Moans of soldiers calling for their mothers echoed through the battlefield. They called out for the one person who was with them at the beginning of their life and now at the end. A legless soldier on his stomach grabbed Uma's ankle and pulled her down.

"Uma, Uma," he repeated. Could she trust herself and allow hope to resurface? "Youngho?" She turned the soldier over.

"I'm sorry," the soldier mouthed. Uma lowered her face closer to his and realized that he was not her son, but the boy who took him away. His baby face hollowed by war, Chung whispered in her ear, "I'm sorry, Uma."

"Where is he?" she asked.

"Youngho," he exhaled.

"Where is Youngho?" she demanded shaking him.

"I'm sorry" were Chung's last words.

"No," Uma shrieked. "Not Youngho."

Apa grabbed her arm, but she tore away. She frantically turned over more bodies. *No, no, no. He can't be dead. No, he has to be alive. He's going to become a famous builder, marry a daughter of a wealthy family who will give him many sons. I will rule the household,* she thought. Uma doubled over, unable to breathe, as fire spread through her chest.

FROM ABOVE, A BLACK snake slithered through snow. At ground level, a mile long trail of refugees marched ant-like with their bounty. Old men and women crumbled to the ground, resigned to their fate. Uma tripped over a frozen bundle of pink as she fought a blustery headwind. She staggered a few steps forward, stopped, and then was blown back. An invisible hand blocked her progress. Apa had difficulty standing and limped with great effort. Sunny took one agonizing step in front of another with her head down holding Nabi's hand. She saw her struggling parents a few feet ahead of her. Nabi plopped down on the snow.

"I'm hungry," she whined.

"Get up," Sunny ordered.

Nabi did not budge.

"I said get up, now!" Sunny hollered. She grabbed the back of Nabi's coat and shook her.

"My foot hurts."

Sunny knelt down and examined Nabi's foot. The sole of her shoe had torn off and her foot was white with frostbite. When Sunny took off her scarf, the angry wind cupped her ears, enclosing her in a chamber of silence. She wrapped Nabi's torn shoe with her scarf. "Now, get up."

DAYS LATER, A UN jeep headed straight for the line of refugees. Fearing the worst, Apa grabbed his daughters and shielded them with his body. A UN soldier with protruding nose and blue eyes reached into his duffel bag. They ducked for cover. Silver stars filled the sky. Nabi squirmed away from Apa's embrace and joined the other children to see what it was. "Cho co lat! Cho co lat!" they cheered. Sunny and Nabi jumped to catch the flying Hershey's Kisses and *gompong*, Korean oyster crackers. Sunny caught a few and gave them to her sister. Nabi took off her mittens and unwrapped the chocolate with her fumbling fingers and placed it in her mother's mouth. Uma didn't bite down; she wanted to savor it, allowing the creamy chocolate to melt on her tongue as the sweet, tangy burst gingerly flowed down her throat. She didn't know what to think. One day the UN bombed them, the next day they gave them candy. Hunger and exhaustion simplified priorities. Food trumped all.

MOONLIGHT WAS NO MATCH for the blinding blizzard. Uma couldn't even see her own hand in front of her. She dodged the refugees' discarded valuables that they could no longer carry on their journey: a chest of drawers, a sewing machine, a phonograph, pottery, books, and clothes. It took all the energy she could muster just to carry herself another step further. Apa kept heading towards the sea; Uma didn't know where to go, she just followed. A gust of wind blew her white scarf off her head. She chased after it, tripped, and fell on her face. The scarf, now a ghostly mask, began to laugh at her. Apa tried to help his wife up, but she didn't want to get up. Uma just wanted to lie there. Frozen. The scarf danced through the night sky and disappeared.

THE NEXT DAY, THEY arrived at a deserted seaport town. The stars twinkled around the full moon. Apa sneaked into an abandoned house and then motioned his family to join him. He built a fire in the stove and Nabi peeled off layers of clothing and wandered into the next room to explore. Uma heard her sneeze. When Uma found her, Nabi's face was covered in white powder. "Uma," she called out. Against the wall sat a twenty-pound bag of US Army flour. They rejoiced in their good fortune as Uma and the girls baked buns. They giggled and danced covered in flour. The girls devoured the buns and Uma took a bite of real food for the first time in days. She turned to her husband and he gave her a weak smile. She had forgotten how handsome he was when he smiled.

AS THE SUN ROSE over the ocean, Uma followed her husband and the girls and rejoined the line of refugees at the dock.

"What's that?" Nabi asked her father, pointing to the UN transporter ship looming ahead.

"It's a LST, a Landing Ship Tank.

"Are we going to get to ride in it?"

"Yes, we are," Apa said and pinched the tip of her nose. "I got your nose."

Nabi checked her face and said, "No you don't, you're silly." She laughed as a child should.

Hours crept by. Finally, the LST's huge door lowered and refugees began to board. Just as Apa was about to step onto the plank, an American soldier with chestnut-colored hair blocked his way. "Mighty sorry, this here one is full. Y'all hafta wait for the next one," he said.

They had no choice but to wait.

THAT NIGHT, ANOTHER SHIP pulled up. Apa sighed with relief. He gave Nabi's hand a squeeze. A fighter jet roared above and bombed the dock. Communist soldiers attacked the ship; UN soldiers returned fire. Bullets zinged overhead. As an American soldier escorted Sunny and Uma onto the slippery ramp, Sunny lost her footing and fell. When the soldier turned to grab her, he was shot in the back and fell into the icy sea. The instant Apa stepped forward to help Sunny, a wave of hysterical refugees pushed and shoved to board the ship, fighting for their lives. The mob pushed ahead, knocking people off the plank. Apa lost grip of Nabi's hand and she was trampled by a sea of refugees. Apa desperately searched for her. He spotted a little girl with her hair in two braids like his daughter, but it was not Nabi. He screamed her name until he was hoarse. The ship was about to pull away. Desperate refugees jumped onto the platform as it closed. Bodies slid into the water. Apa jumped and hung on to the edge of the door, he pulled himself over and dropped into the ship.

Bodies crammed in; there was a steady buzz of moaning and crying. Apa spotted Sunny and Uma crouched in the far corner. He stepped on an old man's hand getting to them. "Where's Nabi?" Sunny asked. Apa lowered his gaze. Uma felt a vise grip her throat. She could not breathe; she coughed so hard that she choked on her vomit.

Moonlight glistened off his dark skin as an American soldier sang, "Silent Night."

Chapter Two
APA

APA FIERCELY HELD ON to his wife and daughter's hands. They filed off the ship onto Koje-do Island, a UN refugee camp on the southern coast of Korea. They passed emaciated North Korean prisoners of war held behind barbed wire fence. The newest prisoners were stripped and deloused with flea powder. Apa eagerly searched the faces of the POWs lined up inside the fence with a flickering glimmer of hope that his son could still be alive among the over 50,000 incarcerated prisoners of war. They were herded into a large courtyard joining thousands of refugees. Uma stared blankly into space. Not used to the heat, she was flushed and dizzy. Apa sat his wife down under a sparse ginkgo tree unable to provide much needed shade.

Apa and Sunny dug through the UN soldiers' garbage for food. She held up a piece of molding bread and meat covered in dirt. Just as she was about to take a bite, a worm crawled out. She dropped false hope. A naked baby boy with a bloated stomach screeched for his mother. Children begged for food as Apa and Sunny stood in line for a ladle of garbage soup. An old man wore his resilience on his matted beard.

There was no water on this forsaken island. Apa stood in line for hours for drinking water. The delirious refugees mobbed the UN soldier and knocked over the kettle of boiled water, spilling it on the ground. In desperation, Uma followed the refugees into the brown, shallow steam and splashed water on herself. She eagerly drank from her cupped hands.

Sunny held a wet sock on Uma's forehead. Uma jerked back and forth in a delirious dream. She opened her eyes.

"Jinny?" Sunny placed the sock back on her mother's forehead.

"Nabi?" Uma's eyes came into focused recognition. She sighed and turned her head.

APA RUSHED A UN soldier patrolling the docks and grabbed his arm.

"Next boat? When?"

"Get back." The soldier pushed Apa with his rifle. Apa made a shape of a boat sailing across water with his hands. He held his hand out by his waist. The UN Soldier's softened and he shook his head.

"I'm sorry, the last ship out arrived on Christmas day."

Apa turned away and stared out at the ocean. Hope dissolved into despair. He held his elbows against his chest, closed his eyes and let out an anguished groan. "I left my baby girl behind," he yelled. He slapped himself in the face and when he opened his eyes, he saw Sunny's terrified face.

He knew it was time for them to leave, again.

The next day, Apa exchanged his watch with a weathered fisherman for safe passage to Pusan. They left one disaster for another. Pusan was overflowing with starving refugees; there was no one to help them. Everyone was left alone to figure out how to survive. They followed other refugees up to a cemetery on top of a hill and built a makeshift tent with cardboard boxes. Sunny dug through the garbage, but it had been picked clean. There were no guarantees that they would survive to see another day.

APA TRUDGED THROUGH THE northern fields of Pusan in dense fog with two fellow scavengers.

"How much further? We've been at it for days," Apa said.

"Are you sure there will be soldiers?" a man asked.

"There will be soldiers alright. Dead ones, I hope," the lead replied.

The fog played tricks. In the distance they were approaching a small hill. As they got closer, Apa realized it was a mountain of dead soldiers.

As they stripped the uniforms off of rotting soldiers, suddenly, they heard barking dogs and searchlights flashed on. They grabbed the uniforms and hid under the dead bodies. Neither dogs nor soldiers could distinguish the dead from the living and the soldiers returned to their posts. Apa pushed the corpses off and sucked in a breath of putrid air. The men put on layers of uniforms and carried all they could. Three bulging figures waddled back into the fog.

APA TOOK HIS LAST step up to their tent and collapsed. Uma stripped the uniforms off him. Sunny hauled water from the well to boil. Uma washed the uniforms. Sunny stirred the uniforms swimming in black squid ink. Uma mended the bullet holes, giving them a second life.

The next day in town, Apa's mouth watered as he strolled by a woman selling steaming noodles and dumplings. The fortunate few sat in the middle of the sidewalk and got their haircut. He laid down a battered, blue *bojagi*, a square silk scarf on the ground and displayed three uniforms. Refugees longingly stroked them. One of the refugees grabbed a uniform and tried to run. Apa tripped him and took his lifeline back. As the sun set, he wiped the sweat off his brow, having sold the last one.

Apa found the climb up the hill to their tent wasn't as difficult as before. Each step seemed to spring him forward. He opened the *bojagi* and revealed to his wife a small bag of rice and a block of tofu. He gave her a feeble smile.

Uma poured the precious grains into a dented US Army aluminum foil tray that she used as a pot. She rinsed the rice and poured the water out. To gage how much water to pour into the pot, Uma laid her hand flat on top of the grains and poured water until it reached her knuckles the way her mom had taught her. Sunny stoked the fire with a stick, ensuring its survival.

They ate in silence. Apa stared into the distance. The last time they ate rice, they were home.

Bap. For Apa, there was nothing like the taste of freshly steamed rice. Scholars have long maintained that five grains of rice are more important than pearls or jade. Traditionally, rice was served in a metal rice bowl with a lid that kept it piping hot. Apa would put a spoonful of rice in his mouth and then blow on it with quick exhales while keeping his mouth open to cool. When he finally closed his mouth, and took his first bite, the sweet, sticky, tender grains melted his heart. There was no other food that brought him more comfort than a bowl of rice.

AS APA SCANNED THE city of Pusan from their cardboard tent, he realized this was the first time he had allowed himself to fully exhale. He cautiously took in deep breaths, unable to fully trust this moment of rest. When his breathing slowed, he could no longer suppress his memories of the past six years. He had been simply trying to keep alive. He did not have the luxury of carefully unpacking the past and making sense of what had happened.

Born during the Japanese occupation of Korea, Apa only knew what it was like to be treated like a second-class citizen in his own country. Korea had always been a small shrimp in a big pond. Surrounded by China, Russia and Japan, Korea had to fight for its survival to remain a sovereign nation. The face of the enemy kept changing, but their propensity for cruelty remained the same. After thirty-four years of Japanese rule of Korea, in 1944, the Japanese found themselves on the verge of being on the losing side of war.

The Japanese soldiers barged into Apa's house. They searched and destroyed, overturned tables and pulled bedding out of the wardrobe. They went to the backyard and searched inside the empty ceramic *kimchee* jars. They were collecting anything made of metal to be melted for the war effort. The soldiers made Apa dig holes in the back yard until they heard the clink of metal. They found the metal rice bowls Apa had hidden. The Japanese had taken everything: his name, his language, and his country. He was not going to let them take his metal rice bowls too. They were all he had left that were Korean.

The Japanese police took Apa to the station and hung him by his arms. The freshly minted police officer punched Apa's face and beat him with a lead pipe. When Apa regained consciousness, he found that they had untied him and taken off his shoes. The older police officer came towards him with a gleaming surgical knife in his hand. Apa backed himself into a corner, his knees held against his chest. The officer grabbed Apa's left foot and dragged him across the blood stained floor. Apa kicked him in the face. The officer showed no rage. It was all in a day's work. The young police officer held Apa down as his mentor slid the knife under the nail bed and ripped off Apa's toenails, one by one.

Apa screamed in anguish as blood spurted out. An excruciating jolt of pain surged throughout his body and then exploded in his head. He fell with a thud.

They released him the next morning. He dragged his bloody feet across the dirt. Sand lodged in his open wounds. He took one agonizing step after another until he reached home.

AFTER JAPAN'S DEFEAT BY the allied forces in WWII, the victors split the spoils of war–Korea. The Russians occupied the north and the United States occupied the south. Within five years, Apa found himself in another war. At the police station, the Communist soldiers shot down the Japanese flag and they raised the Communist flag.

In war and in life, each side had its own perspective of the truth. Each side, convinced they were on the right side of history, felt justified in destroying anyone who did not speak their truth. But the truth kept on changing.

UN TANKS ROLLED INTO Hamhung, North Korea. The first order of business for conquerors was to replace the Communist flag with the South Korean flag at the police station. Second, they showed the villagers a newsreel projected upon a white sheet.

The South Korean newsreel version of the Korean War:

"On June 25, 1950, the North Korean Communist army invaded South Korea crossing the 38th parallel. Within two months, the Communists occupied ninety percent of the Korean peninsula down to the Pusan perimeter. The United States, along with fifteen allied nations, fought under the UN flag for the first time. With the successful Inchon landing, UN forces charged north to the Korea-Manchuria border."

If only war were that simple.

APA WAS TAKEN IN for questioning. A single naked bulb dimly lit the familiar interrogation room. A UN soldier tapped a baseball bat in his hand. A South Korean soldier paced back and forth. Apa's hands and feet were bound; blood trickled from his busted lip.

"Name your co-conspirators," the South Korean soldier demanded.

"I am not a Communist," Apa said.

"Then why did your son join the Communist Army?" he asked.

"He had no choice, they took him."

The last thing Apa remembered was the soldier's baseball bat swinging towards his head.

The next day, they released him. Outside the police station, a South Korean soldier led a group of a hundred civilians including old men, young boys, and pregnant women carrying picks and shovels. These civilians were lower class, in traditional Korean attire. Apa followed behind at a distance along with other curious villagers. The South Korean soldier ordered the rounded up civilians to stop in the field.

Apa, along with the villagers, stood by and watched and wondered what grievous crimes they had committed. The civilians dug a large trench. The South Korean soldier had them kneel on the edge. He then tied their hands and ankles together. "This is what happens to Communist sympathizers," the soldier said. The South Korean soldiers proceeded to execute each person from behind. One shot to the head and their bodies fell cleanly into the trench. Apa sucked in a breath of air. Silence. The onlookers could not react. Had they just witnessed murder of innocent neighbors or had justice been served? He could not show horror or satisfaction. It was not safe. They were instructed to return home and share what they had witnessed with their families and neighbors.

The villagers scattered. Apa followed a village mother and her distraught daughter. The mother raised her hand and threatened to slap her; the girl swallowed her tears. The boys from her class were accused of delivering messages to

Communist soldiers, in exchange for a stick of chewing gum.

A LARGE CROWD HAD gathered for the presidential rally. Apa and Uma watched Sunny and her classmates lined up in identical black uniforms. They cheered wildly as President Syngman Rhee arrived. Princeton educated with stark white hair, he spoke broken Korean with an American accent.

"Thank you for your warm welcome. I am delighted to speak to you today. With the help of the brave UN soldiers, we have defeated the Communists all the way up to the Chinese border." He chopped his hand up and down in the air with conviction. "The Korean peninsula is finally reunited and will forever remain a democracy. I give you my solemn promise that we will protect and defend the Korean peninsula until our last breath."

Students and villagers cheered *mon-sey*, victory, raising both arms into the air. When Uma raised her arms to join in the celebration, Apa pulled Uma's arms down. As the President's motorcade left, the cheering students proudly waved the South Korean flag.

CHANGE WAS THE ONLY thing that could be counted on in war and life. In December of 1950, with the assistance of a million Chinese Communist forces, the North Korean army forced the UN into a massive retreat.

At the police station, the South Korean flag was lowered and the Communist flag returned. Apa was once again arrested and taken to the dingy interrogation room at the police station. A Chinese soldier used him as a punching bag to get things started. A North Korean soldier in a green uniform with a red star paced back and forth.

"Are you a teacher?" the North Korean soldier asked.

"Yes."

"Then you are an intellectual plotting against the Supreme Leader, Kim Il Sung."

"No, I'm not."

"Name your co-conspirators," he said.

"I am a Communist, my son even joined the Communist Army," Apa said.

"Then why did your daughter wave the South Korean flag at the presidential rally?"

APA WAS HELD IN a barn overnight along with over two hundred civilians. Their crime was their livelihood.

They were professionals, business people, politicians, civil servants, artists, and educators. Dressed in western attire, they were the upper class, the elite. A North Korean soldier handed Apa a shovel. Apa's breath rose like a smokestack as he made each icy step. The prisoners were herded to a nearby field and ordered to dig. The shovel was no match for the frozen ground. Apa hadn't made much progress until a man with a pick loosened the ground where he attempted to dig. A North Korean soldier became impatient and ordered them to kneel in front of their shallow graves. "You elitist pigs must pay for your defiance to the Supreme Leader, Kim Il Sung," he bellowed.

Apa bargained with the spirits. *Please, my family needs me. If you will let me live, I'll devote my life to keeping them safe*, he prayed. Apa heard machine gun fire coming from the other end of the line. The North Korean soldiers had acquired more efficient toys of destruction. Then the boom of fighter jets and artillery fire rained down. The North Korean soldiers were caught off guard and ran for cover. The prisoners dispersed. Apa ran past the bodies of civilians in the trench. The machine gun was more efficient, but not as accurate as a bullet to the head. He saw movement among the corpses.

APA FELT AN INSISTENT hand nudging his shoulder. Startled, he grabbed the offending person's wrist.

"Apa, you're hurting me," Sunny said. Apa's eyes refocused on his daughter's face. He realized he was safe in Pusan. He rubbed Sunny's wrist and patted the ground next to him. She hesitated but then sat down. Father and daughter gazed over the city of Pusan. Shoulder to shoulder, they contemplated their uncertain futures.

Chapter Three
SUNNY

A DECADE HAD PASSED since the beginning of the war. Seoul, the capital of South Korea rose from the ashes and its inhabitants did what they had to do to return to normalcy. Some merely survived while others thrived.

Sunny wore a form-fitting button-down argyle sweater, plaid wool skirt, nylons and high heels. A late bloomer, she filled out nicely at age twenty-four. She just graduated with the class of 1960 from Ewha University, and upon her mother's insistence she took graduate level how-to-be-a-wife courses. In western culinary class, she learned how to make petite cucumber sandwiches for high tea. Her teacher, Lydia Kang who lived in England during the war, cut and discarded the brown crust leaving only the fluffy, white center. When it was Sunny's turn to make the sandwiches, she snuck a piece of crust into her mouth. She always thought the crust had more taste. In sewing class, she learned how to make western dresses like the kind worn by Vivien Leigh and Elizabeth Taylor.

WHEN SUNNY GLIDED INTO her father's bookstore, Apa greeted her with a surprise.

"Did it come?" she asked. Apa handed her a package wrapped in a blue *bojagi*–a square silk scarf. In her excitement, she fumbled with the bow and made a tight knot. Frustrated, she handed the package back to her father, like a little girl needing help opening a jar. He smiled and with expert fingers untied the knot for her. "Ibsen's *A Doll's House*," Sunny exclaimed, "I've been waiting for over a year to read this." She squeezed his arm. "Thanks, Apa, you're the best."

He concealed his pleasure with an order. "Make sure you come home and help your mother with dinner."

"Yes sir," Sunny said with a salute.

SUNNY LEFT KYRO BAKERY munching on an adzuki red bean bun with her nose buried in her new book, when she plowed into two American GIs.

"*Yeobosheyo, agassi*–Hello, young lady," they said bowing. Sunny tried to step around them but they blocked her way. The soldier with a carrot top and pockmarks on his face grabbed her arm. Her book and her bun tumbled to the ground.

"We just wanna get to know ya better," he slurred as he leaned in. A foul mix of alcohol and cigarettes lingered as he planted slobbery kisses on her cheek. Sunny pushed his face away and kicked him in the knee. The other soldier held her arms behind her back and laughed while carrot top rubbed his knee and considered his next move.

"Let go of me," she demanded, twisting for freedom. Then she heard the roar of a motorcycle.

"Hey, leave her alone," the driver in English. A tall, leather jacket clad man threw off his helmet. He was a broad faced Buddha with large earlobes. Even in his reproach he seemed serene, untarnished by fate.

"Hey, Hanjin," the other soldier said, letting go of her arms.

"Are you OK?" Hanjin asked.

"You know these jerks?" Sunny demanded.

"They're actually pretty nice guys when they're sober," he said. She rubbed her arms and turned her back to him and picked up her book. The soldiers sauntered on, seeking their next victim. Sunny started to storm off.

"Wait, wait just a minute, I'll be right back," he said, urging her to stop. As he ran into the bakery, she began to appreciate the view from behind. Long strides of a stallion, a man going places.

"Here," he said, handing her a bun.

"Thanks."

"You're welcome." He held up his bun like a glass of champagne for a toast before taking a bite. Pleasure spread across his face like it was the first time he ever had one. He savored each sweet mouthful, fully present, all his attention right here and now.

"No, I mean thanks for helping me," she said, staring straight into his kind eyes. He turned away, embarrassed.

"Oh, it was nothing," he said, and returned to his bun.

They stole quick glances between bites of curiosity. Hanjin kept opening his mouth to say something and then closed it. Finally, he asked, "How would you like to go to a dance on Saturday night?"

"A dance?"

SUNNY LIVED WITH HER parents in a two-room flat above the bookstore. She opened the rice paper door to the main room just enough to poke her head in and wished

Uma and Apa a good night. Apa stared blankly into space. He was having another bad night. All of a sudden, he picked up the fly swatter and swung it in the air. "No, get away," he screamed cowering with his arm protecting his face. He pulled his knees to his chest and covered his toes with his hand. Uma grabbed the fly swatter and slapped it on the table. Without missing a beat, she went back to her embroidery. He reverted to stone. Sunny slid their door closed and returned to her room. With her bulky woolen coat, she barely fit out the window and down the fire escape.

INSIDE THE GYMNASIUM, THE Army jazz band played 'In the Mood' by Glenn Miller. Over fifty couples were on the dance floor swinging to the music. American GIs, South Korean soldiers, and American and Korean Army personnel danced with garishly dressed Korean women majoring in excess. Too much, too tight, too loose.

Sunny had on a simple, yet elegant, beige sleeveless Jackie Onassis-like dress with matching silk pumps, purse and gloves. She panned the room and saw people laughing, drinking, dancing, and having a grand time. She unfolded her handkerchief and placed it on the chair before she sat down. *How could I have been so stupid? I don't know a soul here. I don't belong here. Those women are plastering themselves against their men. I can't do that. No, I have to leave,* she thought. Sunny got up and a golden haired GI held out his hand asking her to dance. She shook her head and sat back down. He got on one knee and pleaded with his hands in prayer. Sunny had never seen eyes like his before. They changed from light jade to aqua blue depending on the tilt of his head.

"There you are," Hanjin said, "I've been searching all over for you." He offered his hand and Sunny grabbed it and rose from the chair. Hanjin shrugged his shoulders and smiled at the GI.

"Wow, you are beautiful," Hanjin said.

"Thank you," she said with an approving smile at the dapper young man in white dinner jacket and black slacks.

"Come on, let's dance," he said, leading her onto the dance floor.

"But I don't know how."

He put his right arm around her waist, and placed her left hand on his shoulder. Then he held her right hand lightly on top of his. When he pushed forward with his upper body, her arms collapsed. "Push back so we have a strong frame," he said. "One and two and back step." Hanjin slowly led the basic swing step. "Lean right, lean left, and back step," he repeated. Sunny focused on her feet and tried to follow. She couldn't keep up with the accelerated beat of Elvis' 'Hound Dog' and mangled Hanjin's toes.

"I'm sorry," she said, stopping.

"You're doing fine," he said, starting the swing again. This time, she felt more comfortable. Right, left, back step. She repeated the steps in her head while mouthing them. Just when she was getting the hang of it, he raised his left arm and guided her in a turn. He was in full command of this dance.

A circle of dancers formed. The band cranked 'Rock Around the Clock'. Each couple sauntered into the circle to strut their stuff. A couple started kicking the Charleston, another twisted and turned, ending in an aerial lift. Another ground their pelvises as Sunny felt her chest flush. The crowd went wild. They cheered the dancers on, moving to the beat as time stood still.

The lights dimmed and the band serenaded them. They swayed to the music at arms' length. The songster crooned 'Love me Tender'.

Sunny felt the heat from his body. Beads of sweat trickled down his temples. When their eyes met, he smiled and pulled her closer. She rested her head on his broad chest, his heart thumped in her ear.

She gazed at his face, his eyes lightly closed, peaceful. Cheek to cheek. His five o'clock shadow poked her tender face like pain that felt good. To give her cheek some relief, she turned her face towards him. An uncontrollable urge invaded her body and she found herself pressing her lips against his. In shock, she pulled away. "I'm sorry," she said, backing up. After a quick recovery, he pulled her closer and gave her a soft, gentle kiss. Blood coursed through her body and pooled between her thighs.

SPRINGTIME IN SEOUL TRANSFORMED accumulated uneasiness into newly blossoming courage. In the spring of 1961, thousands of student-led protesters filled the streets of Seoul. They marched toward the Blue House, Major General Park Chung-Hee's new residence. His successful military coup delivered him his new title: the President of South Korea. Sunny and Hanjin chanted "Democracy Now" and held their Anti-Military Rule signs high. Sirens rang to the backbeat of clanking boots. Riot police with protective masks, shields held high, marched toward them like a steel wall. Blinded by tear gas, the once peaceful demonstrators charged. The police extinguished the explosion with fire hoses. Fists and clubs met flesh.

Some stayed and fought; others attempted to flee. Sunny couldn't move. Packed in like sardines, she trampled over bodies. Trapped. A policeman beat a young co-ed with his club; she screamed bloody murder. Hanjin grabbed the policeman off the girl.

"So you think you're some kind of hero, do you?" the policeman growled as he and his buddies ganged up on

Hanjin, beating and kicking him. Shots rang out. Students and police scattered in the mayhem.

"Hanjin, Hanjin!" Sunny searched in desperation. Broken bodies littered the street, each indistinguishable from the next. At last, Sunny found Hanjin lying in the gutter, curled up in a fetal position. She held his bloody head in her lap. "Hanjin, I have to get you to a hospital." He moaned, shook his head and mouthed, "Home."

UNTIL THAT NIGHT, SUNNY had never set foot in the Chosun district, home of entertainment houses. Rows of *kiwa-jib*, clay tiled roof houses, once only for aristocrats, lined the muddy road. Two businessmen swaggered by with their arms around each other's shoulders serenading the moon. Hanjin stopped in front of a red wooden gate. Sunny unlatched the round metal handle and the rusty hinges moaned. The U-shaped house had a courtyard in the center with a lotus pond and a flowering chestnut tree enclosed by high walls. The slant of the blue roof tiles drained away rainwater and dripped on a limestone boulder. As they passed the main parlor, women dressed in bright silk *hanboks,* traditional dresses, poured drinks for businessmen. They were *gisaeng,* "flowers that can understand words," professional entertainers who sang, danced, and recited poetry for wealthy male patrons. An aging *gisaeng* fed a piece of fish *jun* to a fat, greasy, client who hungrily chomped it down while groping her breasts.

A tall beauty with porcelain skin, red lips and deep-set eyes sat in the back tuning her *gayageum*, a twelve stringed harp. She wore an indigo-purple *chima*, a skirt and a white *jeogori*, a traditional short jacket with long sleeves with two long ribbons tied to form the *otkorum*, the bow. The full-length *chima* with high pleated waistband was tied above the breast flowing over the rest of the body, completely hiding the female shape. She sighed. Her sigh was filled with *haan*, suppressed anger, unexpressed grievance and resentment. Hanjin urged Sunny to move on and pointed to the back of the house. His tiny room with *ondol*, heated floors, was bare except for two futons and a small, low, circular table. She laid him down on the futon and asked, "Where's your *nuna*, older sister, Mina?" An exquisite voice singing of lost love wafted into the room. Hanjin closed his eyes and turned his head towards the music. A tear rolled down his blood caked face.

Sunny helped him take off his shirt and his pants. She had never seen an unclothed male body before. She tried not to touch him but she couldn't help it. His chest was broad with sparse hairs and his muscular biceps twitched. His stomach muscles contracted each time he winced in pain to breathe. She soaked a rag in a copper basin filled with warm water and dabbed the blood off his face. When she squeezed the rag, trickles of blood permeated the once clear pool of water.

"You better go, it's late," Hanjin said.

"Are you sure? I can wait for your sister to come home."

"No, go."

As Sunny passed the foyer, the tall, beautiful *giseang* she had seen before mouthed, "Thank you."

THE RICE PAPER WALL between her parents' and her room held secrets. Sunny could hear the gentle roll of Apa's snore, as she lay in her room unable to sleep.

She had gone to the bathhouse before coming home. It was so late she was thankful there were only an old *ajima* and a mother with her toddler son there. Sunny soaked in a large pool of painfully hot water and then scrubbed every part of her body with a pink sandpaper-like washcloth. She washed her hair three times but she still didn't feel clean. Hanjin's blood had soaked through her skin to the bone.

Even though they had been seeing each other for only a few months, she felt like she had known him all her life. In his arms, she felt safe. Thoughts of him seeped throughout her body. She kicked off the *ibul*, bed covers with her legs and raised her nightgown to her belly. She rubbed her inner thigh with her hand reaching ever closer to the bottom elastic of her panties.

A scream of terror from the next room jolted Sunny from her exploration. Apa was having another one of his nightmares. "Hold my hand, Nabi, we're almost there," he urged. "Oh no, where is she, where's my baby daughter?" he demanded.

SUNNY CLIMBED IN HER bedroom window having just seen her favorite movie, 'Gone with the Wind' for the sixth time. Her favorite scene was when Scarlett O'Hara stood in front of war torn Tara and declared, "As God as my witness, I'll never be hungry again." Sunny imagined the dashing, yet dangerous, Rhett Butler swooping her up in his strong arms and carrying her up Tara's spiral staircase. The possibility of having her very own Rhett Butler became more real in the past months ever since Hanjin entered her life.

"Sunny, get in here right now," Apa hollered. Uma cleared three teacups from the table as Sunny entered the room and sat down on her heels, head lowered. Apa towered over his daughter. With his hands on his hips, elbows turned out, and eyes narrowed, he was in no mood for sweet talk.

"Where have you been?" he demanded. Sunny had learned from past experience that silence was the best strategy. "You knew he was coming." She wiggled her toes to keep them from falling asleep. "We waited for you for three hours." Apa jabbed his fingers in the air.

"I'm sorry," Sunny mumbled.

"Why are you trying to bring shame upon this family?" She didn't dare move. Her father's anger had only one setting–full blast. He forcefully lifted her chin to make sure she understood. "We're going to meet him at a café with his parents next week and you *will* be there." Sunny pleadingly turned towards her mother who deflected her gaze and continued to pick imaginary lint off her blouse.

THE MATCHMAKER THOUGHT SHE had made an extraordinary match. She analyzed their compatibility on three critical factors: social economic status, education, and height. Marriage was serious business, a merging of two families. The parents pre-screened the potential spouse and then set up a *seon*, an arranged meeting of the candidates.

He sat with his ankle resting on his knee, elbows outstretched, and hands clasped behind his neck. A freshly lit cigarette burned in the overflowing ashtray. Tewon Kim, thirty, licensed pharmacist, youngest son of a high school principal. He sat humming to himself.

"This is my daughter, Sunny," Apa proudly said and pushed her towards Tewon.

"Nice to meet you." Tewon rose from his chair and bowed. Sunny bowed back. They stood eye to eye. She now understood why Uma insisted that she change out of her high heels and wear flats. He was slight with delicate features, a narrow face, large, intense eyes hidden behind wispy bangs. He was pretty. Apa gave his daughter a hopeful smile and returned to the parents' table.

"Please, sit," Tewon said. A waitress came to take their order. "Get me a shot of Johnny Walker Black," he said dismissively.

"We don't serve alcohol," the waitress said, shaking her head.

"What? Two black coffees then, make sure it's piping hot," Tewon said.

"I'll have pine nut tea, please," Sunny interrupted. They sat in silence. She crossed her ankles and arms. Tewon touched his nose and scratched his neck. When their drinks arrived, he gulped his coffee in one swoop and slammed the cup on the saucer with unsteady hands. He lit another cigarette and noted the time.

Finally, he said, "You graduated from Ewha University."

"Yes."

He blew smoke in her face. Sunny coughed. He fanned the smoke and put out his cigarette.

Then lit a fresh one.

THE RADIANT FALL COLORS engulfed the happy couple as they drove through the countryside in Hanjin's new jeep. As he accelerated through the curves, they squealed like children, laughing until their bellies ached. Sunny found her hand grabbing his thigh as they jolted over a bump. With reins firmly in hand, the charioteer delivered his precious cargo to the foothills of Namsan Mountain, which once marked the southern edge of Seoul many generations ago. An old stone fortress remained on guard.

They strolled hand in hand under gingko trees while chewing on grilled squid. The smell of chestnuts roasting filled the air. Hanjin stopped at the vendor and bought a bag. Sunny peeled the crunchy skin and popped a perfectly roasted chestnut into Hanjin's mouth. When she tucked her hair behind her ear, she brushed her cheek with her hand that had the remnants of charred chestnut skin. Hanjin gazed at her face and smiled. "What, what's wrong?" Sunny asked. Hanjin gently rubbed the black mark from her cheek with his thumb. "I couldn't be happier." He peeled another chestnut and savored it. Warm and sweet. Pure comfort.

Fat squirrels hurried along preparing for harsh times ahead. When Hanjin and Sunny reached the summit, they could see the entire city below. Hanjin laid out a blanket and unwrapped the green *bojagi* revealing a bento box. He popped a piece of *kimbop* into Sunny's mouth. She wondered how so much flavor could be packed into such a small package. Crunchy carrots, daikon, spinach, salty soy sauced ground beef, sweet fried egg, vinegary white rice all rolled up in seaweed. The colors of the five elements: fire, earth, water, metal, and wood were surrounded by white symbolizing purity, integrity, and chastity.

"I wish we could stay up here forever," Sunny said.

"We can." Hanjin reached into his denim pocket and took out a gold band. "Sunny, will you marry me?"

"Really?"

"Really."

"But—" Hanjin interrupted with a kiss.

"We can do it. I know we can," he said eagerly nodding. Sunny laid her head against his chest as he held her from behind. *Could this be happening? A husband, love, safety? Do I dare hope that happiness can be mine,* she wondered. Sunny flashed Hanjin a smile then turned away. She bit her lip and swallowed the sour taste of nausea.

UNABLE TO CONTAIN HIS desire to begin a life with Sunny, Hanjin called on her parents the next week bearing a basket of fruit. Apa and Uma positioned themselves on one side of the divide. Hanjin and Sunny performed a full prostration bow, a sign of veneration and respect. They dropped to their knees, then leaned forward on all fours, and then sat back on their heels while their heads touched the floor.

"I'd like to ask for your daughter's hand in marriage," Hanjin said with his head bowed. Sunny couldn't protect him.

"What!" Apa leaned forward into Hanjin's space and opened fire.

"Where are your parents?"

"I escaped south with my sister during the war," Hanjin replied.

"Which college did you graduate from?"

"I own a delivery company and I am taking electrical engineering classes at night."

"You don't even have a college degree and you are here asking for my daughter's hand?"

"I will complete my degree next year," Hanjin added.

"Where do you live?"

"In the Chosun District with my sister."

"Where the entertainment houses are?" Apa pounded his clenched fist on the table. "How dare you, you *geseki*, you son of a bitch, insult me like this?" He raised his hand to slap Hanjin.

"Apa, no." Sunny grabbed her father's arm.

Hanjin rose to leave. She pulled at his pant leg, urging him to sit down. He turned away and stormed out.

"How can I give you to an orphan?" Apa said in a softened tone.

"Nabi's an orphan too," Sunny snapped back. Apa slapped her. She held her stinging cheek. Apa grabbed her hand and squeezed so tight that she couldn't pull away. Uma opened the fruit basket and bit into an apple.

HANJIN AND SUNNY MET at Diamond Mountain restaurant. He picked the tenderest part of the fish's belly with his chopsticks and placed it into her rice bowl as a peace offering for the previous day.

"I couldn't stay and let him insult me that way," he said.

"But you could have let him get to know you better," she argued.

"His mind was made up."

"More than you know," she said, shaking her head.

"What do you mean?"

"Apa has chosen my husband through a matchmaker. He even went to the fortune teller to make sure we're compatible."

"That's nonsense, fortune tellers don't know if we're compatible, only we know," he said.

"Apa just wants what's best for me, to be well taken care of by a wealthy family."

"I can take care of you," he said earnestly. "We can rent a small room by the university. I know it'll be a struggle at first, but we can make it. We'll be together." He reached over and held Sunny's hand. "Can't you see us growing old together? A house in the mountains, me playing with our grandchildren and you painting your landscapes?"

"Father has suffered so much."

"We all have," Hanjin said with sadness in his eyes.

"He's already lost two daughters and a son. I'm all he has left."

"Sunny, I love you, we can make it."

"How can I live a happy life when others have perished?"

"Because others have perished, that's precisely the reason why you must live an extra happy life for them."

"Is love enough?"

"It has to be," he said. Sunny pulled her hand away.

"It's easy for you to say; you don't have any parents to defy." As soon as those words fell from her lips, she regretted it. A pained expression spread across Hanjin's face as if she had punched him with her words. *I don't deserve this—love is not for me. It will never work out,* she thought, yet she couldn't deny the truth of her heart. She knew what she needed to do.

SUNNY AWOKE WITH THE roosters to prepare Apa's favorite, *jeonbokjuk,* abalone porridge. She sliced the abalone and sautéed it in sesame oil. Next she added soaked rice, water and simmered it for half an hour. She added a pinch of salt and ladled the white, creamy porridge into jade green ceramic bowls. She brought in her most potent weapon in her arsenal and placed it in front of Apa. He folded his paper and they ate in silence.

"Would you like some more?" she asked in a sugary tone. Apa placed his hand over his bowl.

"Hanjin just secured the government contract. He'll be hiring five more employees," she said with a pleading smile.

Apa was unmoved. "He can't help that his parents are in North Korea. You know that. His father was a doctor."

Apa slammed his hand on the table. The jade bowl teetered for balance and crashed on the floor.

"*Shikoro*, you ungrateful girl. How dare you question my judgment! You will obey and marry whom I choose. I forbid you to ever see him again."

Sunny couldn't shut up as her father commanded.

"But Apa," she sobbed, "I love him."

"We can't afford such a luxury."

SUNNY FOUND HERSELF DRESSED in a wedding gown riding to the wedding hall in a black sedan. Dazed and numb, she felt herself floating outside of her body watching herself go through the motions. The past month had disappeared in a whirlwind of activity. The sedan stopped at the entrance of the wedding hall. She sat, unable to move. She absently gazed out the window and then she saw him.

He was unloading cases of *soju* from his jeep. He rolled the Korean vodka on a dolly to the entrance and peeked inside the hall where over three hundred guests waited. He returned to his jeep for another load.

Sunny stepped out of the sedan and paused. She stared at the jeep, lifted her veil one last time.

Hanjin leaned against his jeep and saw her. Stunned recognition jolted him. Wedding music began. Hanjin headed towards her. His pace quickened.

Sunny pulled down her veil and proceeded into the wedding hall.

FOR TWELVE LONG YEARS, Sunny endured. She had chosen the well-worn path taken by women for centuries. She kept her head down, suppressing any outward expression of her true feelings in favor of maintaining a façade of support. Each day melted into the next. How could it be 1973 already, she wondered. Cooking, cleaning, dusting, washing, over and over again; even though they lived in a tiny, postage-sized room above her husband's pharmacy in Seoul, it was never clean enough. After the day's duties were done, she savored the few moments at night when she allowed herself to think about the past.

Sunny lay on the futon on the floor and stroked her daughter's thick hair. Every time she inspected her six-year-old's pudgy face, she saw her baby sister, Nabi. Guilt clenched her heart with every beat. Sunny instinctively pulled her hand away. Her father's sudden death still shocked her. How could he be here one day and gone the next? Last summer, Apa started complaining that Uma made his food too spicy. He got to a point where he couldn't hold down any food, no matter how bland. By the time he saw a doctor, it was too late. The cancer had spread from his stomach to his liver.

Apa lay under several blankets, shivering. Sunny held his hand, trying to hold back her tears.

"I'm sorry," he whispered.

"Apa, I'm sorry," Sunny said.

"Nabi. My poor baby girl. You have to find her."

"Yes, Apa, I promise."

He died three weeks later. Sunny felt empty. Her rock, her dad, was gone. Loneliness seeped into her heart. When Hanjin's face surfaced in her mind, she pushed it down with all her might. A chill ran down her back.

"*Shibbal*" Tewon swore as he tripped over his wife and tumbled onto the futon. Sunny raised her index finger to shush her husband and pointed to Lydia. Tewon loosened his pant buckle and pulled down his drawers. Then he lifted his wife's nightgown, pulled down her white bloomers, grabbed her breast, and smacked his lips making loud popping sounds. She shushed him again. "Come on, make me a son," he said. Sunny turned her head and lay there like a corpse. He was limp and could not enter. Seconds later, he fell on top of her and gave up.

Trapped beneath him, Sunny tried to steal a breath of air. He relaxed his arms and let her feel the full force of his dead weight. She jerked her body from side to side until she rolled him off her. Tewon landed with a thud.

"It's all your fault," he said. She said nothing. "You make me drink," he baited her. She knew her silence was louder than words. "You dried up bitch, if you can't please your husband, the least you can do is give me my son." She just stared at him with burning eyes. She felt her rage bubbling up, but nothing came out of her mouth. "Are you mute? What do you have to say for yourself, you worthless piece of shit?" He shook her shoulders. "I can divorce you," he threatened. She released a faint mumble, "Go ahead." He raised his hand to slap her but she ducked, and his fist slammed onto the table. As he nursed his bruised hand, he repeated his favorite Korean proverb "Women and chickens need to be beaten three times a day." After all, women lived with the forgiveness of men.

THE NEXT MORNING, WHEN Tewon awoke, not a trace of his drunken night was visible. He had on his pajamas and his hair and body were clean. His wife had closed the pharmacy for the day and his breakfast was ready.

She made him a morning after soup called *haejangkuk* made from beef bone, dried outer cabbage, and clotted ox blood.

"A woman came by asking for you," Sunny told him.

"Who?"

"She wouldn't tell me her name. She said she'd come back later."

"What did she have on?"

"A pink feather boa."

Tewon suppressed his smile.

The phone rang; Sunny answered. "Again? Yes, I will come get her. Thank you."

NOW THAT SHE WAS a widow, Uma had no one to take care of. She was finally free to do what she wanted.

Dressed in her white mourning *hanbok*, Uma got off the bus at the DMZ (Demilitarized Zone), with a small bundle tightly held against her chest. Tourists were on the observation deck. The tour guide explained that the border between North and South Korea had nearly two million troops deployed on both sides including 37,000 U.S. troops. Beyond the barbed wire fence, a wildlife sanctuary flourished. Within the 250 kilometers by 4 kilometers corridor, wild habitats had rebounded from war's destruction. Endangered and rare animals and plant species had found homes. The land between had been untouched by humans for almost twenty years. The tour ended and Uma stood by the fence. She opened her bundle and grabbed a fistful of cash. She shoved it in the face of a South Korean soldier.

"I'm going to see my daughter in North Korea, here, take this," she said.

"No, ma'am," the soldier said, refusing her bribe.

"I'm going to see Nabi," she repeated.

"You will have to step away from the fence," he warned.

"You can have all this," she said, offering her bundle of cash. The soldier radioed his counterpart.

"The old lady's back, please call her daughter and put her on the bus," he said. A female South Korean soldier escorted Uma.

"Old lady, go home," she said.

"I am going home," Uma replied.

UMA PULLED THE STOP requested lever and got off the bus near the DMZ. The bus driver asked her if she was sure she wanted to get off there, and she told him that she was going home. She shuffled to the barbed wire fence and faced north. With her bundle tied to her waist, she climbed the fence. An American soldier at the DMZ patrol tower spotted her through his binoculars. He climbed down the tower and ran towards her.

"Stop, stop right there," he yelled.

The razor sharp wires shredded her hands. Even though her hands were dripping with blood, she felt no pain. With peaceful determination she continued to climb. She held on with one hand as she reached into her bundle.

"Hold it right there," the soldier ordered, firing a warning shot in the air, startling her. Uma fell backwards. A pool of blood formed around her head.

At first observation, a flock of birds flew in the breeze, but upon closer scrutiny, one hundred *won*, Korean bills, swirled in the wind landing safely in no man's land.

Chapter Four
TEWON

TEWON HAD SPENT THE evening drinking with his brothers.

The Korean word for alcohol was *Sul*, a combination of Chinese characters *su*–water and *bul*–fire. *Sul*–fire water. Tewon's first drink, at age fourteen, was *makkoli*, unstrained rice liquor, the drink of farmers. When he spit up his first swallow, his brothers laughed at him and repeatedly slapped his back. He expanded to *soju*, a 20-30 proof distilled vodka-like liquor, inexpensive and powerful, an easy solution to life's troubles. He was glad he was a slow flusher instead of those weak bastards who turned bright red after one drink.

Tewon hated the discomfort of the unknown. With a few drinks, his anxiety was coated with a layer of false charm, where he became Superman, Clark Gable, and Gandhi all rolled into one.

In each interaction, Tewon had to determine where he stood on the social hierarchy and who deserved respect. His twin brother was born minutes before him, but Tewon still had to call him *hyung*, older brother, when his brother called him Tewon.

Hyung offered Tewon a glass. He received it with both hands. Hyung poured and Tewon drank with his head turned to the side. When Tewon returned the favor, he cupped his right sleeve with his left hand as instructed when pouring for a senior. Tewon's job as the youngest was to keep all the cups full. The brothers drank and ate appetizers called *anjoo*, dried beef, dried cuttlefish, squid, nuts, and fruit.

Tewon offered a drink to a stranger passing his table. When he declined, Tewon hollered, "Afraid to show your true self?" The stranger shook his head in disgust. Tewon couldn't trust a person if they hadn't drunk together. Throughout the night, he and his brothers fought, argued, laughed, and boisterously sang.

By the time Tewon got home that night he was sober. He clearly hadn't drunk enough. He thought he saw one lump instead of two on the floor, but he couldn't be sure and he didn't care. He plopped down on the bedding. He thought he heard something downstairs, but he closed his eyes.

TEWON AWOKE TO A loud crash of glass breaking and a thump coming from his pharmacy. He picked up the first weapon he could find, a fly swatter, and tiptoed downstairs. "Who's there?" he called out.

The light from the pharmacy created dancing shadows. Tewon peeked inside and saw bottles of drugs strewn about. He tiptoed into the pharmacy and peered behind the counter. Sunny, in white mourning *hanbok,* covered in blood and dirt, lay there with a satisfied grin on her face. There was an empty bottle next to the wall among broken glass. He shook her. "Sunny." She was unconscious. He struggled to lift and carry her out. He had to rest several times before they arrived at the clinic down the street.

The doctor, still in his pajamas, pumped Sunny's stomach. Tewon held her hand.

"I'm sorry. I promise to stop drinking if you come back."

Sunny spit up the pills and vomited.

"That's a good girl, one more time," the doctor said. Sunny opened her eyes and Tewon hugged her.

"Sunny," he said, relieved.

She felt dejected that she had failed even at this. She closed her eyes.

"Thank you for saving her life, doctor," Tewon said, shaking the doctor's hand with both of his.

"I should have insisted that you come with her when I told her the test results."

"What results?"

"She didn't tell you?"

"No, I haven't seen her since morning."

"She has a blockage in her fallopian tubes from an infection."

"What does that mean?" Tewon asked.

"I'm sorry, she cannot have any more children."

TEWON SWEPT THE FLOOR of the pharmacy before anyone could see the evidence.

"Tewon," a lavishly dressed woman said, "it's me."

"I didn't recognize you," Tewon said.

"I came by earlier and your maid said you would be back later."

"She's my wife."

"Oh, of course, I'm sorry," she said. "So you became a pharmacist after all."

"Yeah, as my father wished." They stared at each other until he deflected her gaze.

"We were a great duo," she said.

"The best."

"Remember Myung Dong Nightclub?" she asked. "The crowds loved us."

"The crowd loved you."

She began to sing and he joined her in perfect harmony. They laughed and each took a bow.

"Did your father ever prove that his opponent stuffed the ballot?" she asked.

"No, but his senate campaign cost us our house. The bastards repossessed and demolished it to build high rises."

"Now his son has a respectable wife—" she paused "-that should win the people over." Tewon gave her an uneasy smile. "I want you to meet someone. He's waiting outside," she said. He followed her out.

"This is my son," she said. The boy was about five years old. He was leaning over, playing with a top. Tewon's heart jumped into his throat.

"Hey, what do you have there?" he asked. The boy turned his head towards Tewon. His features were Eurasian.

Tewon smiled at him and mussed his hair. Disappointment and relief filled his heart.

"He's been coughing up blood. The doctors near base treat us like we're from outer space. I thought you might know a doctor," she said. Tewon nodded.

TEWON SWUNG HIS LEGS back and forth on his favorite barstool. He had kept away for three months.

"Hey Tewon, I haven't seen you in here lately," the bartender said. "Welcome back, the usual?" Tewon hesitated, and then nodded. The bartender brought him whiskey on the rocks. He twirled his index finger around the rim and lifted the glass to his lips. His hand started shaking and he slammed the drink down on the bar.

THE OIL CRISIS HIT Korea hard. People were forced to choose between food and medication and most chose food. There were days when Tewon did not have a single customer at his pharmacy. When a customer would come in, they would insist that Tewon give them the medication for free. When he refused, they would curse him.

The previous year, Tewon met with his college buddy who had immigrated to the United States right after college. He told Tewon that the United States was desperate for doctors, nurses and pharmacists due to the Vietnam War. Since the passing of the Immigration Act of 1965, which abolished national origin quotas, it was easier for Koreans to immigrate to the United States.

"I know all about the Vietnam War, Dad," his daughter said. "We made cards in school for the Korean soldiers fighting in Vietnam."

"We're going to fly on a plane and move to America," Tewon said.

"We're moving, Mom?"

"I just have to pass an exam to qualify and repeat my graduate work," Tewon said.

"With his English?" Sunny thought aloud.

WITH BOTH OF HER parents gone, Sunny felt there was nothing left for her in Korea. She stared out her plane window, hopeful at the chance to start over–to pursue the American dream.

TEWON SAT IN THE lecture hall of the University of North Carolina with his tape recorder. He scribbled some notes, and then broke his pencil in two. The sound coming out of his professor's mouth was gibberish to him.

SUNNY'S ENGLISH WASN'T ANY better. She interviewed for jobs but she couldn't understand the questions being asked. Her degree from one of the top universities in Korea was meaningless in America if she couldn't speak English.

Sunny stared at the residents in wheelchairs and walkers at the nursing home. She asked the receptionist for an application and then waited as instructed.

When Sunny entered the manager's office, she noticed a Korean War Veteran plaque hung on the wall.

"I see you have a college degree. Are you sure that you want a nurse's aide position that pays minimum wage?" he said.

"English poor. Need work."

The manager gave her a tour.

"Why old people not home with son?" Sunny asked.

"Their children can't take care of them."

THE NEXT DAY, A black nurse's aide was undressing an old white lady for a bath.

"Your hands are dirty," the old lady said.

"They're perfectly clean," the aide replied.

The old lady screamed bloody murder just as the manager and Sunny entered the room.

"What's the matter?" he said.

"She's touching me with her dirty hands."

"Sunny, take over."

The old lady stared at Sunny. She touched her hair, face, nose, and eyes.

"How can you see out of them eyes?"

The old lady took Sunny's hand and compared it to her own.

"Your hands are clean."

"Sunny, she's all yours."

TEWON'S DAUGHTER CRIED EVERY morning when he dropped her off at school.

"I don't want to go," Lydia pleaded.

"You have to so you can be smart."

"I don't know what they're saying."

"Just smile and nod like you understand," her dad advised.

A group of blond, blue-eyed children advanced toward her. Lydia ducked.

"They're going to kill me."

"Don't be silly."

"I saw them on TV, they kill Korean children with their blue laser beam eyes."

"Go, I'm going to be late." Tewon pushed her out of the car. Lydia held up her book bag to block the rays and ran inside.

CHUCKIE, A NINE-YEAR-OLD Korean American boy, sat next to Lydia. He had on a white shirt, blue pants, and red suspenders.

"Don't you know that plaid pants and a striped shirt don't match?"

"What meaning?" Lydia asked.

"Speak proper English."

"Hey, Chuckie, she your girlfriend? You two have the same chinky eyes." The bully howled and pulled his eyes back with his fingers.

NO ONE SAID IMMIGRATING to America was going to be easy, but Sunny was unprepared for the sudden loss of ability to speak and comprehend language as soon as she landed in America.

She couldn't have imagined the difficulty of transitioning from a homogenous country where everyone spoke Korean to a nation of immigrants from all over the world who spoke English.

Just surviving each day was all she could barely manage. One day at a time.

Lydia, sitting in the back seat, stuck her head between her parents.

"Where are we going?" Lydia asked.

"To a birthday party," Sunny said.

"Whose?"

"America's. It's 200 years old."

"It's just a baby. Korea is thousands of years old," Tewon said.

EVEN FILLING UP THE gas tank was a challenge.

"Fill her up," Tewon said.

"Three dollars?" the attendant asked, holding up three fingers.

Sunny leaned over and tried. "No, fill me up," she said. The attendant was taken aback. Tewon shook his head and held up both hands, fingers wide. Sunny handed him a ten-dollar bill. Transaction completed. They drove off. Sunny and Tewon laughed; Lydia joined in. As laughter faded, 'This Land is Your Land' played on the radio. Fireworks began as Lydia waved the American flag out the car window.

SUNNY HAD BEEN MOVED to the cafeteria to help serve Thanksgiving dinner. She scooped mashed potatoes onto a tray and another nurse's aide ladled the gravy.

Sergeant, a former WWII POW, screamed.

"This Jap's poisoned my food."

"Calm down, Sergeant, no one's done nothing to your food."

"You sneaky Japs."

"I no Japanese, I Korean."

"You gooks are all the same."

He threw his tray at Sunny. A fork flew up and cut her forehead. He lunged at her and she fell.

"Attention," the manager ordered.

Sergeant rose and saluted. The manager reached out a helping hand to Sunny and she accepted.

BY THE SECOND YEAR of graduate school, Tewon had to choose between paying tuition or feeding his family. Because all of the real estate values were depressed when he sold the pharmacy in Seoul, he wasn't able to bring as much cash as he wanted when they came to America.

One of his classmates told him that in California, he would just have to pass the licensing exam without repeating his graduate work. Tewon dropped out of school and worked in a pharmacy as a stock boy while he studied for his exam.

"You open it," Tewon said.

"No, you open it," Sunny insisted. They went back and forth until she gave in and tore open the envelope with the test results. Tewon lit a cigarette and inhaled. Sunny shook her head.

"I can't take it anymore. Why did we ever come to this godforsaken country?" He crumpled up the paper and tossed it. "We can go back to Korea and start over. The economy in Korea is improving. We can start a drug store," Tewon said.

"We came for Lydia," Sunny said. "So she can have a good future."

"She's only a girl," he said.

"Just take the exam one more time," Sunny pleaded.

Tewon lit another cigarette.

TEWON NEEDED AN EYE opener to get going in the morning. He brushed his teeth and rinsed twice with mouthwash. He stashed mini-bar sized bottles of whiskey in his locker at the hospital, just in case. He had finally passed his licensing exam and moved to San Jose, California eight years ago. He was a pharmacist for the county hospital dispensing medication, but he couldn't get through the day without a drink. The more he snuck around to drink, the more he drank to cover up the bad feeling that he was drinking again.

One drink after work ended up to be a drunken night of partying. Tewon and a fellow pharmacist clinked glasses of whiskey after they bought a hundred shares of a hot start-up company. Unfortunately, Sunny found out.

"You touched our savings!" Sunny shrieked. "I've been saving that money to go to Korea to find Nabi."

"I know, I wanted to invest it, so you can go sooner," he said.

"How could you risk my money?"

"So, it's only *your* money?"

"I've been saving for decades."

"You have no faith in me, you never have."

A WEEK LATER, TEWON bragged, "See Sunny, I told you so, we've doubled our money in a week. You'll be able to go to Korea in no time." His stocks just kept on going up and up. "I don't even know why I work as a pharmacist when I can just buy stocks and make money. It's so easy," he said.

His high came tumbling down on Oct 19, 1987, Black Monday. The stock market crashed and the DOW plunged 508 points.

"Where have you been?" Sunny asked.

"We've lost everything. The start-up went belly up" Tewon said.

"What?"

"But we can buy more stocks and win it all back," he said with confidence.

"Are you crazy? Do you know how many years I've been saving that money?"

"Now's the best time to buy low," he said.

"You're pathetic."

ANOTHER YEAR HAD GONE by without his notice. Tewon lounged on his Lay-Z-Boy lounger in his underwear. He hadn't shaved, left the house, or taken a shower in days. He barely ate. The fan blew in his face. Bags of potato chips, pieces of dried squid, and peanut shells were scattered about. Several empty Johnny Walker bottles rolled on the coffee table. He was singing 'Love, Love Me Do' when Sunny stepped in.

"What are you doing?" she demanded.

"I'm just having a party by myself," he said.

"You promised to search for a job. You promised to send out your resumes. You promised to quit drinking."

"That was a long time ago, Sunny dear," he replied.

Tewon poured a shot and handed it to her. She stood there with her hands on her hips.

"How come you never drink with me?" he asked as he drank her shot.

"Good thing Lydia isn't here to see this."

"Sign this," he said, handing her the papers.

"What have you done now?"

"We can take a second mortgage and buy more stocks. We can win it all back and more."

She tore the papers and threw them at him. Tewon chugged from the bottle. Whiskey ran down his neck, choking him like a vise.

Chapter Five
LYDIA

EVEN THOUGH SHE DIDN'T like turkey, Lydia's mother made it every Thanksgiving to show her patriotism. She insisted on getting a twenty-pound turkey even for three. "We don't want Americans at the grocery store to think we're poor boat people," her mom said. She rinsed the pale bird three times with hot water, sprinkled it with salt and pepper and rubbed the skin with butter. She threw the neck out for her daughter's protection. "If you eat the neck, you'll crow like a rooster and no man will want to marry you," she warned.

She soaked the sweet rice overnight. The steam from the rice cooker pulsated like heart chambers filling with blood, lifting and dropping the aluminum lid. She peeled the onion, rinsed it three times under cold water, and then cut it in half. She cut vertically through the onion half from the flat base to near the root end, careful not to cut all the way through the root. "See, it's like the handle of a comb holding the teeth together," she said as she cut horizontally across the vertical teeth, producing precise quarter inch square onions. The celery, carrots, mushrooms, and beef were diced to her exacting standards. Only the frozen peas were immune to her blade.

The hot oil popped and sizzled as she lightly sautéed the vegetables and meat with soy sauce. She never measured. She just knew. She added the vegetables and meat to the sticky sweet rice with a pinch of salt and pepper. She drizzled the sesame oil last so that the rice could absorb the spices. She slapped her daughter's hand if she tried to help. Lydia stood at attention like a soldier. She didn't utter a word, just observed. Her mother pointed her head towards the kitchen utensils drawer and Lydia had the honor of handing the scalpel to the surgeon.

Her mom's secret ingredient for her stuffing was chestnuts boiled in sugar. The one and only time Lydia got to peel the chestnuts was when she was in sixth grade. Her mother had just worked the morning shift at the nursing home and prepared the turkey at dizzying speed. Having forgotten to boil and peel the chestnuts the night before, she made a crisscross cut on the flat side of each chestnut and then dropped them in a saucepan with two inches of water. After the brunettes bobbled for twenty minutes, she rinsed and drained them three times in the yellow plastic strainer she got at Mrs. Chun's Tupperware party.

38 Chestnuts

The chestnuts burned Lydia's tender hands as she tried to work quickly. For the first few, both the smooth outer shell and the brown inner skin peeled off together. In between chestnuts, she put her burnt fingers on her earlobes as she had seen her mom do, but it didn't bring her any relief. As the chestnuts cooled, the outer shell came off easily but the inner parchment stubbornly hung on. When Lydia took a butter knife and tried to scrape off the inner skin, the two halves broke. When she got all the chestnuts peeled, she proudly handed her mom the bowl.

"Can't you do anything right?" she shrieked as she grabbed the bowl out of Lydia's hands. "That was the last of the chestnuts." She turned her back to her like a fortress and proceeded to stuff the awaiting bird. She placed one spoonful of sweet rice stuffing in the cavity. Next she picked up two halves of a chestnut, placed them together and poked it into the stuffing. "We'll just have to fake wholeness this year," she sneered.

THEY PROMISED TO KEEP their undies on. Lydia was on top. Her long hair hung down like vertical blinds, allowing in flickers of light as she spread her arms, and flew. She inhaled Philip's musty, sweet, tangy scent, and licked the surf salt streaks off his neck. Quick light kisses followed by deep hunger. Their pelvises met as she rubbed against him with the full force of her body weight. She unhooked her black Wonder Bra and unleashed her breasts in his face. His calloused palms squeezed her buttocks. His fingers led him to the well. He rubbed his creamy fingers as she bit his lips and tasted hot, tangy espresso. She gazed down at her breasts and rolled back and forth against his lower abs, locked in crunch position. Crash of cymbals, jolt of contractions, warm tingle spread throughout.

In measured decrescendo, her body disintegrated into space, no beginning, no ending, suspended, held in trust, free.

Lydia fell on top of him. His carotid artery thumped in her ear. She turned her head and stared at the pulsating vein on his neck and made a note to herself. *That's where you stab a person if you want them to bleed to death,* she thought.

Ring, ring . . . ring, ring . . . ring, ring . . *What the hell?* She rolled off him, careful not to fall off of the dormitory issue single bed. Ring, ring. She sauntered over to her desk and picked up her beige Trimline phone.

"Hello?" she answered.

"Lydia?"

"Yeah, mom," she said, annoyed by the interruption.

"What took you so long?"

Lydia muffled her laughter as Philip flashed through his best Calvin Klein underwear model poses.

"I was busy."

"Don't be late for our first Thanksgiving dinner alone."

Lydia kicked her leg as Philip licked her toes. "I'm bringing–a friend," she said cautiously.

"Who is she?"

"He... his name is Philip." Dead air filled the line.

"What's his last name?"

Lydia eyed his eager face but turned away.

"Philip Namu ... uh ... Nammm," she mumbled into the receiver. He dropped her leg and shook his head. "Gotta go, see you on Thursday," she said in a hurry.

LYDIA GREW UP IN a cookie-cutter suburban home outside of San Jose. A tan house with beige wall-to-wall carpeting, the window shades remained closed to discourage the curious. Lydia scanned the living room. The clunky, fake crystal ashtray sat on the end table by his brown corduroy La-Z-Boy. Teetering piles of Korean videotapes were stacked on top of the television. The TV, VCR, and stereo remotes stood by in a faded Christmas card box. Her dad hadn't taken a thing. "Cuckoo," the bird called, jarring Lydia, making her jump. It was the first extravagant purchase he made when they moved into this house. He proudly displayed it above the TV. A Swiss chalet cuckoo clock with Roman numerals and pine cone weights made of cast iron. The relentless tick of the pendulum bob. The wooden cuckoo that emerged to call out on the top of the hour. Lydia wondered why the call hadn't bothered her when she lived there.

The Formica kitchen table in dress whites barely poked through. Proudly polished silver chopsticks and a spoon with royal blue Chinese lettering sat next to each of the avocado green flowered Corning Ware dinner plates. Lydia never knew what the Chinese characters meant and she wondered what the sage Chinese calligrapher in the park wrote for real when he offered to translate your name in Chinese for a dollar. Wide mouth drinking glasses, large enough to fit her fists, were filled with cooled boiled water. Light pink baby carnations arranged in a crystal dessert bowl took center stage.

The once pale bird now back from the tropics sported a perfect golden glow. Savory soy soaked sweet rice stuffing beamed with whole chestnuts. A bowl of pungent Napa cabbage kimchee fermented with garlic, ginger, red pepper, sugar and salted shrimp shared the table with a bowl of cubed daikon kimchee, unknowingly mistaken for canned pineapple chunks by Korean food novices. Slick jellyfish salad with shrimp, cucumber, and Asian pear marinated in vinegar and sugar with a bite of hot mustard and garlic was a challenge even for expert metal chopstick users. And last but not least, jellied cranberry sauce on a plate, still in its canned form.

"Great turkey, Mrs. Kim, very moist," Philip mumbled between mouthfuls.

"It's a little overcooked, don't you think?" Mom cued Lydia's protest.

"The sweet rice stuffing is my favorite," Lydia said taking another heaped scoop. Her mom snatched the stuffing bowl away from her and placed it in front of Philip.

"Philip, where do your parents live?"

"In San Francisco. I grew up there."

Lydia attempted to grab a piece of daikon kimchee but it slipped between her metal chopsticks and fell back into the bowl.

"What do they do?"

"Dad is a professor and Mom is in real estate."

"My father was a teacher too," Mom proudly stated.

"I thought he owned a bookstore," Lydia inquired. Mom silenced her with her all too familiar girls are to be seen, not heard glare. Lydia returned to her duel with the daikon kimchee and stabbed it with her lance.

"Your parents must have come to the United States when they were young."

"They were both born here," Philip said. With a quizzical expression on her face, Mom took a swig of ice water and patted her moist upper lip with her napkin.

"Will you pass me the stuffing? Lydia sweetly asked Philip, nodding her head in anticipation. She slapped another heaping glob on her plate, creating a fortress. Then she used her spoon to carve a moat and filled it with gravy. She picked up a whole chestnut and dipped it in the moat and then popped it into her mouth, "umm, umm," she crooned. Mom shot her a disgusted scowl and then instantly returned to her artificial smile and turned to Philip.

"Do you speak any other languages besides English?"

"*Si, Hablo Español. La cena es muy deliciosa,*" Philip suavely delivered.

"Muchas Gracias, Señor," Mom answered.

Philip helped himself to more jellyfish salad; Mom proceeded with the interrogation.

"Do you have any brothers or sisters?"

"An older sister. She has two adorable girls, ages three and five."

"She must be planning on having more children. Doesn't her husband want a son?"

"No, they're happy with their girls." Philip turned to Lydia and beamed. Her mom's eyes darted back and forth as if she was watching a tennis match.

"What are your plans after graduation?"

"We've both applied to MSW programs."

"And then you'll go on to get your PhD," she declared.

"Lydia, we should invite Mr. and Mrs. Nam over for dinner sometime."

Philip gave Lydia a stern warning as she shook her head and squirmed in her chair. A mixture of dread and overeating made her feel queasy. He turned to her mom and said, "Mrs. Kim, my parents are Mr. and Mrs. Namura."

A burning sensation raced up from Lydia's stomach to her throat, leaving a foul acidic taste in her mouth. She covered her mouth and took a deep breath.

"What!" Mom exclaimed in disbelief. Her face turned molten red. Eruption was imminent. She jumped out of her chair and slammed her hands on the table and knocked over the kimchee bowl. Lydia frantically blotted the red kimchee juice with her napkin to try to avoid it staining the white tablecloth, but it was too late.

PHILIP SLEPT ON HIS side facing his girlfriend with his mouth ajar. His legs twitched like he was running from something; his breathing quickened to a pant. Then, all of a sudden, he exhaled with a sigh, mumbling something about bears. He had been holding her for six hours. His only break was to pick up six-packs of Kleenex, cherry flavored Tums, and Kit Kat bars. His taut abs rose and fell like a metronome. His eager brown eyes turned up towards the left with his mouth pinched. His mind raced a mile a minute and he struggled to think of something, anything, to say to her. He opened his mouth and then closed it. Surrendering to the moment, he relaxed his furrowed brow and held her tighter.

They met freshman year in Professor Wong's Asian American history class. The slap-slap of flip-flops grew louder as Lydia reviewed her notes one last time before the exam. *Focus,* she reminded herself. "Over forty-eight distinct Asian American and Pacific Islander groups live in the United States, each with its own language, culture and history," she repeated. *Uhh, what's that smell? A mix of salt, sweat, and donuts,* she mused. He plopped down next to her and flashed a Tom Cruise smile. Spiky black hair with blond streaks, a jagged scar above his left eyebrow, tan, cut up shoulders in baby blue OP tank top with black QuikSilver surfer shorts.

"Hi, I'm Philip," he said as he extended his hand.

"Lydia," she replied placing her hand in his. The grit of sugar lingered on her fingertips.

PHILIP SPENT EVERY SCHOOL break in Hawaii with his Tutu, aunties, uncles, and a dozen cousins of varying hues. At Haleiwa, he and his cousins practiced the ancient Hawaiian sport of the gods. In the winter, they faced some of the largest waves in the world.

Surfing was how he learned to simply be. In the early mornings as the sun awoke, he paddled out into the azure blue ocean on his long board. With aching arms, he sat facing the horizon, watching, waiting. Creatures of the ocean brushed against his legs as he sat in relaxed alertness. With no sense of passage of time, he floated in the warm, glassy ocean, safe, at one with the world. Then the wave approached. As the energy accelerated, he greeted it. When he rose onto his board and peeled through the waves, he was focused and present. Each one was different, every moment new.

After a day of surfing, Philip and his cousins stopped at Auntie Kalei's drive-in for some ono grinds. Philip started with one of his favorites: Spam musubi–fried Spam marinated in shoyu and sugar, with rice wrapped in nori, dried seaweed. Then he followed up with a plate lunch. In Hawaii's plantation days, workers of different ethnicities shared each other's meals to create plate lunches with food from different countries combined on one plate. A plate lunch consisted of two scoops of rice and a scoop of macaroni salad with the main meat on top. Philip's favorites were Korean Kalbi Ribs, Japanese Beef Teriyaki, Hawaiian Kalua Pork, Filipino Chicken Adobo and Chinese Char Siu Pork. Other favorites included hamburger steak smothered in brown gravy, beef stew, and curry. He topped it off with shave ice, a soft powder of ice that was far superior to a mainland snow cone with flavors such as lilikoi passion fruit, haupia coconut with li hing mui powder made from dried and salted plums. Sticky sweet juices ran down his arm as an ice cream headache tingled his nose.

LYDIA COULD NEVER FORGET the first time she had dinner at Philip's parents' home in San Francisco. Jason and Janet Namura lived in a Victorian house on California Street. The exterior of their home was painted in bright blues and greens with pink trim. Philip removed the sourdough bread he had baked from scratch from the oven. Steam rose as he tore off a piece. He swirled it in a mixture of balsamic vinegar and extra virgin olive oil and placed it in Lydia's mouth. The sour, tangy explosion caught her by surprise. Philip shot her a satisfied grin at her pleasure. What Lydia loved most about him was that he was comfortable in his own skin. And when she was in his home, she felt comfortable in hers.

Jason Namura was born in the Poston Japanese internment camp in Poston, Arizona during WWII. His parents and three older brothers, all U.S. citizens, were forcibly removed from their home and incarcerated along with 110,000 Japanese nationals and Japanese Americans. President Roosevelt signed Executive Order 9066 that mandated the incarceration of anyone who was of one-eighth or greater Japanese ancestry. It was a precarious time for Americans who had the face of the enemy. President Roosevelt signed no such order for German or Italian Americans, only Japanese. Upon release after three years, his family became even more American to show their patriotism—only meat and potatoes for this 110 percent American. To that day, Philip's dad preferred eating with a fork to chopsticks.

Janet Namura's family had been in Hawaii since 1885 when the first contract laborers came from Japan. During WWII, most Japanese Americans living on the Hawaiian Islands were not interned due to the fact they represented one-third of the population. She was the first girl in her family to come to the mainland for college.

Philip's parents were college sweethearts whose adoration for each other permeated their bright and airy home. He blew on the spoon to cool his famous olive spaghetti sauce and offered it to his wife to taste. With a saucy kiss she sealed her approval. As Lydia carried two plates of spaghetti to the table, Philip followed behind repeating "Ve are goinck to pump," clap, "you up," while transitioning through bodybuilder poses with a strained facial expression. When the slippery noodles slid onto the floor, his parents just laughed, real laughter, the kind with snorting. When his mom finally caught her breath, she said to Lydia, "No worries, we got plenty."

GROWING UP, LYDIA TRIED to be away from home as much as possible. When she was home, she was in a constant state of high alert, waiting to find out what else she had done wrong.

Each day, her mother conducted her daily ritual of prewashing, washing, rinsing, folding, and hanging with exact precision. Not a single note was out of tune, off beat, or held too long. She washed the plastic hangers and dried each one, making sure that she never dropped one onto the carpeted floor. Each load of laundry could only contain one type of clothing. But before the clothes could be placed in the washer, they had to endure their private punishment for their sin of having been worn. The collars of her husband's shirts had to be scrubbed by hand to remove the dirt left by his neck. His socks had to be soaked and scrubbed together to remove the stink of his feet. The front and rear portions of his underwear had to be scrubbed to remove any stains left by careless wiping or aggressive gas. Each load was washed three times. First, the rinse cycle, then the wash cycle with detergent, and then a second rinse cycle. Even the towels followed this regimen even though they had only been used once to dry a freshly cleaned body. The laundry could only be folded in one place, on her bed. The comforter and the flat sheet had to be lifted revealing only the fitted sheet. The towels were folded lengthwise and then in threes. All the shirts in the closet faced left, the top button closed.

Her four sponges lay in their proper places next to the sink, one to soap the dishes with, one to rinse the dishes with, one to clean the table with, and one to clean the stove with. The dishwasher could never be used since it didn't do its job well enough. The chopsticks had to be washed with the pointy ends facing down. All dishes were dried naturally, never hand dried even with a clean dish towel. Everything was in its proper place, like soldiers standing at attention for their next command. Don't touch, don't move.

HER MOM SAID THAT a happy family ate together. The evening meal was a lesson in composition. All four food groups had to be in balance. All five colors—red, white, black, green, and yellow–were complementary yet distinct. Each bite was a complex yet simple combination of sweet, salty, sour, bitter, and savory.

Wednesday was not Prince Spaghetti Night at their house, it was flounder night. Flounder was Dad's favorite, it reminded him of his childhood in Korea. The flounder in his memory was no bigger than the palm of his hand; it was no surprise that the flounder in America was giant like everything else. Mom scored the whole founder five times, sprinkled with salt, and let it sit for three hours. To prevent the fish skin from sticking to the grill, she pierced holes through the skin with a toothpick. Then she broiled the fish for ten minutes per side. Next she spooned the soy sauce seasoned with sugar, rice wine, garlic, ginger, and sesame oil over the fish and put it in the oven for two minutes.

Lydia carefully set the table making sure that the head of the spoon and the tips of the chopsticks did not touch the table but hung off a small side dish. Then she called her dad to dinner.

Lydia and her mom sat at the table, smelling the delectable scent of garlic and ginger as their stomachs growled. Just when Lydia felt like she couldn't resist taking a bite, her father sauntered into the kitchen holding a crumpled *Korea Times* and turned on the TV to *World News Tonight* with Peter Jennings. The females sat quietly in anticipation of his first bite, for the eldest male of the house had to start eating before anyone else could. He twisted open his Miller Light and gulped the entire bottle before coming up for a breath. Then he went on to the next bottle. "Drink on an empty stomach to get the full effect," he lectured. "Drink first, eat later, if you have to." After his fourth bottle, he cracked a sinister grin and picked up the tenderest part of the fish's belly with his chopsticks and placed it in his mouth.

"*Shibal*," he swore and spat the fish on the table. "It's cold." Mom rushed the fish back in the oven.

Lydia felt her face flush as she blurted out, "All you do is complain about the food, why don't you cook it yourself?"

"How dare you question me, you ungrateful *gijibae*?" he demanded. He slammed his fists down and his chopsticks rolled off the table.

"Mom, sit down and eat, you're not his maid, you know. Like you haven't worked hard all day too."

"Eat. I'll be right there," she said, giving her the evil eye to settle down. Her dad reached into his shirt pocket and took out a pack of Kents and lit up. As Lydia stormed out of the kitchen, coughing, she faintly heard her mom say, "I'm sorry."

AFTER SHE LEFT HOME for college, Lydia rarely returned. In the beginning of her senior year, her mom called to tell her that she had filed for divorce. She didn't offer a reason; she didn't need to. Lydia would have divorced him ten times over, yet she wondered what pushed her over the edge. What did he do or not do this time?

A few months later, her dad came to ask Lydia for money. He shuffled in his Nike plastic slippers. Neither his greasy comb-over nor his aviator sunglasses could hide his middle age blues. In green-checkered shorts belted below his beer belly and turned up collar Izod shirt, he leaned in for a hug. His whiskey breath took her back to when she was a child. His nightly ritual consisted of rubbing his whiskered face against hers and then sitting next to her bed and watching her for what seemed to be hours. She pretended to be asleep. She eventually fell asleep to the sound of his breathing.

AN ENTIRE SEMESTER HAD gone by since Thanksgiving. Lydia called her mother and told her that she was coming home for a visit.

She wandered into the freezing house. Eerily silent. The red digital alarm clock blinked from its place on top of the TV. The couch was covered in a white sheet with freshly laundered towels on top. Mom fanned herself. She wore her house clothes, a white undershirt and a skirt she had made from a purple flowered dress that she wore during her pregnancy. They sat down on the couch, across from each other. Mom pulled on her wooly sweater and then within minutes took it off.

"Lydia, you really should lose weight and what have you done with your hair?" Mom picked up another bath towel, folded it systematically in half lengthwise and in thirds.

"Mom, I have to talk to you."

"I see you haven't been using the thigh master I got you for Christmas."

"It's important." Lydia picked up a towel and folded it her way.

"We can go to brunch tomorrow. It's not every day a woman crosses the half century mark." Mom beamed.

"Mom, listen," Lydia deplored. "Philip and I are going to live together at U of M."

"Not the Japanese!"

"Philip is not Japanese. He's an American just like me."

"Lydia, there are so many Korean families wanting to introduce you to their sons. They are doctors and lawyers, very successful. You can have the pick of the litter."

"His dad was born in an internment camp during WWII. We stripped them of all their possessions and made them live like cattle locked up in pens."

"They deserved it." She rose and put on her sweater.

Mom said, hovering, "Don't you know what the Japanese did to the Korean people? For thirty-five years they tried to eliminate the Korean culture–our language, our way of life. I had to change my name to Noriko to attend school. We were punished for speaking Korean. We had to become Japanese."

"But Philip didn't have anything to do with the Japanese occupation." Lydia put her hands on her hips.

"Japanese men are the worst. They treat women like animals," Mom said, hovering. "How can you love a Japanese? His blood comes from the same devils." She sunk down in her chair, refolded Lydia's towel. "If only you knew what they are capable of–"

Lydia ripped the folded towel from Mom's hands and threw it on the table. "I am very aware of the history... who did what to whom. How long must the next generations keep hating?"

"You don't know what happened."

Mom pinched her mouth, took a deep breath and exhaled.

"He makes me feel whole, safe to be me." Lydia stood.

"I forbid you." Mom stood.

"It's not your choice."

"Then your father will decide."

Lydia laughed in her mom's face. "Just stop with your Confucius bullshit—a woman's lot is to be subservient to her father, husband, and son. Where has it gotten you?"

The frustration, disrespect, and the inability to shame her daughter raged inside Mom. There was no reasoning with her willful daughter. Perhaps she should have listened to Uma and not had a daughter in the year of the fire horse. She didn't know what else to do to protect her daughter. She grabbed Lydia's hair and threw her to the ground. She slapped Lydia's face, head, and ear with alternating blows.

Lydia didn't know why she was shocked by her mother's behavior. Growing up, at least on a monthly basis, Lydia did or didn't do something that resulted in a beating. Her mother's rage could only flow downward in the family hierarchy, landing on her face. Lydia never cried. She refused to give her the satisfaction. It never occurred to her to hit back or run away. She thought she must have deserved the beating. But not anymore, she knew this was the last time her mother would lay her hands on her. She grabbed her mom's wrists with both hands. Mom struggled to free herself but Lydia was now stronger. She glared into her mom's eyes.

"I will marry Philip."

"Then you are not my daughter."

"This is America. I'll marry the man I love."

Her mom shrunk before her eyes. Lydia knocked over the towering pile of bath towels and stormed out.

TWO YEARS LATER, PHILIP and Lydia were living together in Ann Arbor, Michigan. Crinkled pieces of paper strewn about, research books piled high on the floor, Philip sat at the computer typing; Lydia feverishly edited her Master's thesis. Ring, ring . . . ring, ring.

"You answer it," Lydia told him.

"No, you answer it," he said.

"Answer it," she demanded.

"No, you answer it, you're closer," he argued.

"Just answer the God damn phone!"

Philip reluctantly picked up the phone. "Hello, hello?"

He heard a click on the other end just like the last twenty times he had picked up the phone.

"It's her, isn't it?" she asked.

"You think?"

"I can't deal with her right now."

"It's been two years."

"I can't; just leave me alone."

Philip engulfed Lydia in his arms. She batted him away and tried to shake him loose, but he held her tighter.

The stress of pretending she didn't care finally shot up like a beach ball held under water. As the pressure released, tears of sorrow poured from her eyes.

"You're going to have to talk to her eventually."

"No, I don't."

"Lydia, she's your mother."

"I only need you," she sobbed.

"You have me." Philip pulled a tissue from the box and held it to her nose to blow. Her breathing steadied. She suspected that the emptiness she felt in the pit of her stomach was from more than just hunger. "Have you ever asked your mom about her life in Korea during the war before she came to the U.S.?"

"What does that have to do with anything?"

Philip raised an eyebrow. She should know better than to ask what one's past has to do with one's current behavior.

"She said I was born in Seoul, South Korea, and that we are all from Seoul."

"Was *she* born in Seoul?" Philip asked.

"I guess so, she said she was an only child and my grandparents passed away when I was a toddler."

"Anything else?"

"No, she got all defensive, so I stopped asking."

Philip became quiet.

"What?"

"My dad won't talk about camp either. He tries so hard to blend in and prove himself.

"Isn't he still angry about what happened?"

"War is a cowardly thief."

Chapter Six
SUNNY

S HE HUNG UP AGAIN. She couldn't get herself to talk to him. The Japanese continued to bring sorrow to her life.

She had a name once before she became Mrs. Kim or Lydia's mom. Her name was Sunny before she had wrinkled, cracked hands, raw from washing. She had even been in love once, but her daughter thought she was nothing more than a deaf mute maid. Sunny kept the TV on to improve her 'hearing,' but even after fifteen years in America, the talking heads murmured like men drowning in their own blood.

Uma warned her to be careful not to have a child the year Lydia was born. "It's bad enough that it's the year of the horse, but it's the year of the white yang fire horse. You might have a girl and she'll be wild and uncontrollable," her mother cautioned.

Sunny and her older sister Jinny were banished to their aunt's house when Uma was about to give birth to their new sibling. It was bad luck to have girls in the house during the delivery for fear that another girl would be born. The curse of being born a girl. A disappointment from her very first breath.

STILL, A GIRL SHOULDN'T have to suffer like her sister Jinny. The day Jinny went to the market to buy green onions for Uma, she was picked up by the Japanese police and taken to what the Japanese military called a comfort station.

A tattered Japanese flag hung limply on its pole. Hundreds of Japanese soldiers lined up outside rows of huts. Being young and beautiful was not an advantage. She was first brought to an officer's tent. When he was done with her, she was taken to a hut and thrown on a dirty hemp mat. Screams of terror filled the huts. A Japanese soldier unbuckled his pants. She tried to get up but a twelve-year-old girl was no match for a starving soldier. He pinned her down and locked her hands above her head. He parted her slender thighs with his knees and thrust into her, ripping her open. She screamed. No one came to help. He slapped and pounded her with his fists until she passed out.

The stench of blood, rotting pus of untreated sores, and dried sweat kept her in a constant state of nausea. Maggots, worm-shaped larvae of flies feasted on her open wounds of infected tissue. As one soldier buckled his pants, another unbuckled.

Jinny lay frozen beneath another thrusting soldier. Vacant eyes, slashed face, and broken nose were the aftermath of having been systematically beaten and raped daily. Over thirty soldiers a day, one after another. Jinny heard a gunshot and muffled a cry.

Outside, a pregnant girl lay in the snow. A bullet through her forehead. There were plenty more where they came from. The soldiers didn't care. They were going to die anyway.

AFTER JAPAN LOST THE war, the Communist liberators rescued the comfort women and Jinny returned home.

Uma barely recognized her own daughter. In six months, she had aged twenty years. Jinny was a skeleton of her old self. She had the blank stare of a person whose spirit had been sucked out of her. She wouldn't or couldn't speak.

When Uma hugged her baby girl, she hung limply in her arms. Uma knew that she couldn't provide the comfort her daughter needed. A mother's love was not enough.

The next morning, Sunny found her older sister in the well.

TEWON STOOD IN FRONT of his former home wearing a light blue tuxedo and rang the doorbell. He doubled over and grabbed his stomach. He hadn't been able to keep anything down lately. He couldn't sleep and much of his day was a blank. He teetered back and forth and then grabbed the doorknob to maintain his balance. His ex-wife opened the door in her sweats. Her hair was matted, face flushed. She wiped under her eyes with the tip of her ring finger and then slid her thumb and forefinger down her nose, pausing at her nostrils with a pinch.

"Com'on, Suunn-yy, we hafta go, to the church," Tewon slurred. She scanned him up and down with disdain. With her arms crossed in front of her chest, she stood there for what seemed like hours.

"I'm not going," she said.

"What do ya mean, you're not goin'?" Sunny tried to close the door, but he stuck his foot in to keep it open. "But, she's our only child," he pleaded. She kicked his foot out and slammed the door in his face. Tewon furiously pounded on the door. "God damn it, Sunny, stop being so stubborn."

He peeled out of the driveway. He was already late. He leaned over, grabbed a flask from the glove compartment, and took a swig. When he peered over the steering wheel, he saw that he was heading straight for a mother and her son crossing the street. The boy screamed as his mother flew through the air. Tewon kept driving.

Chapter Seven
LYDIA

PHILIP'S DAD HAD TO give Lydia away at her wedding. Jason said it was his pleasure to give her away because what we give away returns to us multiplied. In contrast, her mother followed through on her threat. They did not speak to each other while Lydia was living in Michigan. After Lydia got her Master's in Family Counseling and Philip got his Master's in Social Work, they could have moved anywhere. Philip insisted that he missed his parents and wanted to be near them. Lydia didn't want to go back, but she knew sometimes you needed to go backwards in order to move forward. The cold war continued even after she moved back to the San Francisco Bay Area eight years ago. Neither mother nor daughter was willing to take the risk and take the first step.

Lydia worked for a county agency that provided social services and counseling for Asian Americans. She saw very few Korean clients. She found that many Koreans were governed by *chae-myon*, where what other people thought of them was paramount. Consulting someone outside the family about their problem was admitting that they couldn't handle it. Shameful. So they kept everything to themselves, bottled up. The stigma and guilt of mental illness kept the secret hidden until it was apparent to everyone except to the patient that they were sick.

Some self-medicated with booze to drown their sorrows, as did Lydia's dad, until his total disregard for other people's lives landed him in the California state prison. His blood alcohol level was at .28 percent, three and a half times the legal limit. He had a suspended license due to three prior DWI offenses. He was charged with second-degree murder and sentenced to fifteen years in prison. The prosecutor argued, "At some point a person's actions are so reckless his behavior becomes malicious. He knew the consequences when he drank and drove and that made it premeditated." Her dad was paying the price for driving drunk and killing an innocent human being.

Lydia knew that no one was all bad or all good. She just chose to focus on the bad, especially when it came to her Dad. He had already served half his sentence and she never went to visit him. He deserved his punishment and she was not going to allow herself to be hurt by her birth parents again. The only way she could deal with them was to pretend they did not exist.

LYDIA AND PHILIP'S HOME was decorated in black and white. Modern, stainless steel cold. Lydia, who had just turned the big 3-0, sat at the kitchen counter and poured herself a glass of wine. Then another. She opened up a pile of bills. A letter from the California State Prison Board.

"Shit."

Philip trudged into the kitchen.

"Hey."

"I'd offer you some wine but it appears there isn't any left." Lydia held the empty bottle upside down.

"You've had enough."

"Don't tell me what to do. I am sick and tired of having to listen to people all day."

"I'm going to bed."

HOURS LATER IN THEIR bedroom, the battle continued.

"You never said you didn't want a child before we got married," Philip said.

"The world is overpopulated," Lydia said.

"We would be just replacing ourselves, we wouldn't be adding."

"Babies are noisy and messy."

"I want a child."

"I don't need an eight pound baby coming out of my vagina to feel complete."

"I think we can provide a good family."

"Mr. 'I had a perfect childhood with perfect parents'."

Philip sighed in defeat, "You only see what you want to see."

Lydia lay awake on one side of the bed; Philip lay awake on the other side. Careful not to carelessly cross the line in the sand, both turned away from each other. They wound themselves tightly and stayed as far as possible away from the line.

WHEN LYDIA GOT HOME from work, she had nothing left–for her, Philip or anyone else. She just wanted to crawl into a hole and disappear. Even eating had to take the least amount of thought or energy. They ate microwaved burritos on most nights except when they picked up take-out.

"What?"

"What?"

"Nothing."

"Fine."

"Fine."

Was this the same man I used to have long conversations with into the wee hours of the morning? Lydia wondered in disbelief. He used to want to know how she felt, every little thing. What she missed most was his tenderness. Now she couldn't even hold a five-minute conversation with him without one of them feeling hurt or defensive. Any attempt to talk ended in stony silence. Not being able to talk to her best friend drove her deeper into despair. She felt afraid of being alone, desperate.

Lydia watched Philip load the dishwasher. He finished and turned it on. Lydia got up and opened the dishwasher and put the cups on top and the bowls on the bottom.

"Fine, you do it," Philip said.

"If you would just do it right, I wouldn't have to do it over."

"You're just like your mother."

"I am nothing like my mother."

Lydia noisily put the dishes back the way Philip had them.

AFTER ANOTHER SILENT BURRITO, Philip sat on the couch and said nothing. He and Lydia sat across the divide. He did not want to engage her. Shut down, head down, she could tell he just wanted to disappear, yet she pursued him, needing someone to blame.

"I hate this house. You made me buy a house we can't afford and now I'm trapped in this crappy job," Lydia said. Philip's arms crossed. One side of his mouth drew back, creating a defiant dimple.

"Don't you have anything to say?"

He stonewalled.

AFTER WHAT SEEMED LIKE an hour, Philip finally spoke.

"I'll buy you out."

"What did you say?" Lydia said.

"I'll buy your half of the house. Go, be free." He waved his arms in the air. "I can't make you happy."

She felt like she had been sliced open. *He's leaving me,* she thought.

"You're willing to throw us out so easily? Do you know what I went through to be with you?"

Philip rolled his eyes and played air violin.

"Yes, you sacrificed your perfect family for me," Philip said.

She had never heard him like this, dripping with sarcasm. Lydia was stunned.

"You're so miserable with me. I'm just trying to solve your problem. And since you think I am the problem, then leave."

"You can't just walk away from us," she implored. "How dare you?" She grabbed his shoulders and shook him. When she let go, he turned back to stone.

A WELL-LIT ROOM, fresh daisies in a cream vase, Monet painting on the wall. Lydia slouched deeper into the couch.

"I hate my life. Why aren't I happy?" she whined. She had been seeing a therapist off and on for the past three years and even Dr. Margaret was getting fed up. She took off her glasses and put them on top of her yellow legal pad.

"Who told you that you get to be happy?" Dr. Margaret said.

"Isn't it in the US constitution or something? Life, liberty, and happiness?"

"There are only three things that are guaranteed in life. You get old, you get sick, and you die. Anything good in your life, you have to put it in yourself. No one's responsible for your happiness except you. Only you."

"Crap."

LYDIA CAME HOME AND poured bottles of liquor down the drain. No more Blue Hawaiians; no more shots of Ouzo; no more Kahlua and milk. She had to pour it all down the drain. She didn't want to be tempted by alcohol—an easy fix. When she drank, she felt happy. Not a care in the world. The more she drank, the less she remembered why she was drinking. She felt good. Before any social interaction, she drank to get prepared. It just seemed easier with a drink. Discomfort dissipated into numbness. That's how she made it through high school and most of college, until she met Philip.

"Biology is not destiny. I can choose another outcome no matter the predisposition of my genes," Lydia tried to convince herself. She poured the final bottle down the drain.

"Good bye, friend." Lydia tore open a bag of Hershey's Kisses. She unwrapped one and popped it into her mouth. She chewed twice and swallowed. Before she knew it, half the bag was gone. She hadn't tasted a thing. She closed the bag with a rubber band. On second thought, she opened the bag and unwrapped another one.

"Mom" was a loaded word for Lydia. Being a mom wasn't a career that she had any training or any interest in. But Philip's biological clock was ticking. Lydia knew he would make a good dad; she, on the other hand, had no delusions about, or confidence in, creating a happy family.

LYDIA RETURNED TO DR. MARGARET'S office. For the past eight sessions, Philip had come with her.

"So, what did you learn?"

Lydia handed the book *Men are from Mars and Women are from Venus* back to the doctor.

"That I'm mostly Martian," Lydia said.

Dr. Margaret smiled.

"How about you, Philip?"

"I need time to be in my cave–alone."

"You are both professional listeners at work, but when you get home, you tune each other out."

Lydia and Philip held hands.

"Practice using your "I" statements."

"I, I, Doctor," they said in union with a salute.

"And when you are feeling anxious, instead of triggering your fight or flight response?" Lydia and Philip rested their hands below their ribcage and took in a deep breath.

"One, two, three," Dr. Margaret slowly counted as she tapped her thigh. They exhaled, for six counts.

"Rest and digest," Philip said.

"Congratulations, you two are officially kicked out of couple's therapy." Lydia and Philip gave Dr. Margaret a hug and smiled at each other.

"Now go home and talk to each other."

Lydia realized that she did take Philip for granted and thought that just because they were married, he would have to stay even if she became unbearable to live with. And Philip was to work on telling her what was on his mind even if he was afraid of her reaction. They both understood that they had choices, choices about how they respond to each other.

LYDIA WORKED IN AN overcrowded county facility, in a low budget, beige cubicle. She crossed off another day on her monthly calendar. A precious day she could never live again. One of Lydia's clients, Mai, a Vietnamese refugee, rushed into her office.

"Ms. Kim, Ms. Kim, I need you," Mai screamed.

"Mai, I'm right here. Calm down." Lydia put her arm around Mai and sat her down.

"Breathe in, breathe out," Lydia encouraged. Mai continued to pant, arms protecting her heart, shivering.

"You help me."

"Of course."

"He get worse, he fired from job, hit boss."

"We'll file a restraining order on him."

"I scare he hurt Jamie."

"You'll be safe."

"They beat him refugee camp. He not same man."

FIVE-YEAR-OLD JAMIE heard her father's '78 Chevy pick-up truck sputter in the parking lot. Mai pushed Jamie into the kitchen cabinet and signaled for her to be quiet and closed the door. There was banging on the front door.

"Mai, open the door."

"Go away or I'll call the police."

"I'm your husband, I order you open this door right now."

He continued to ram the door with the full force of his weight. The chain rattled with each thrust.

"Stop. You hurt yourself," Mai said.

Reluctantly, she opened the door. Her enraged husband grabbed her by the neck.

"You're mine. You can't ever keep me away."

He slammed Mai into the kitchen cupboards. Trapped against the cupboards, she removed a .38 revolver from the drawer.

"Leave, right now," she said as she pointed the gun at him.

"I'll never leave you. I promised to protect you forever."

"Get out."

He lunged for the gun. They struggled and fell to the floor.

Jamie heard a shot. She covered her ears with her hands. Then a second shot.

Lydia followed officers into the crime scene. Her heart sank when she saw Mai and her husband's dead bodies outlined on the floor. She started opening up the kitchen cabinets. She opened the door of a corner cabinet and found Jamie curled up, with knees to chin, arms covering her head.

"Jamie," Lydia said. Jamie tightened into a ball.

"Come on out, it's OK." Jamie would not budge. Lydia reached her hand into the cabinet. Jamie bobbed and weaved keeping out of Lydia's reach.

"It's going to be OK, I promise."

After what seemed like an eternity, Jamie crawled out. Sirens and police officers filled the crime scene. She gazed at the empty outlines of her parents on the floor. When she stood up, she grabbed onto Lydia's skirt and bear hugged Lydia's leg. Lydia unfurled Jamie's fingers from her skirt and then firmly held Jamie's hand in hers. They stepped out together, hand in hand.

LYDIA WAS ONLY A few years older than Jamie when she came to the United States. She didn't even know her ABCs when she was plopped into the second grade. She cried everyday because she didn't want to go to school.

But by fourth grade, Lydia was in the rabbit reading group and spoke perfect English. She didn't know that she had an accent–a Southern accen– until she moved to California.

Her mom brought her to register for junior high school. The counselor glanced at Lydia in her Dorothy Hamill haircut and started speaking to her loudly and slowly.

"We–can–enroll–her–in–English–as–a–Second–Language," the counselor said.

"I reckon I can teach her a thang or two," Lydia said in her Southern drawl.

"My, you speak English so good."

"Well, it's English so *well*," Lydia corrected her.

"The teacher is from Vietnam or something like that and I'm sure you'll understand her just fine," the counselor said.

Her mom lifted her eyebrows and tightened her lips. After years of making Lydia her public mouthpiece, her mom gathered her courage to speak in her daughter's defense. "All honors courses Lydia in. And Honors English," she boasted.

In her junior year of high school, Lydia was co-captain of the cheerleading team. She only hung out with white friends. She tried to be whiter than the white girls. At parties, she got hammered and danced on the tables. After a couple of shots, everything felt easier, she could just let loose.

A fresh crop of FOBs, fresh off the boat immigrants from Vietnam and Cambodia, streamed into her school on a monthly basis. Lydia and her friends were standing by their lockers when an FOB, dressed in rolled up khakis and stained white shirt, navigated towards her. He placed his palms together in front of his heart and made a slight bow.

"Lydia, he likes you," her friends teased, giggling.

That's when she realized why Chuckie was so mean.

IT WAS A BLUSTERY day in Oakland. The winds were fierce and it hadn't rained in months. Lydia answered her phone at her desk at work.

"Yes, I'm her daughter. No, I haven't seen her in years. I'll see what I can do."

Her mom had been working at Jasper Computers assembling microchips since Lydia was in junior high. Her mom wore a white clean suit, completely covered from head to toe like an astronaut. She said the best part of the job was that everything was so clean.

Lydia was listed as her emergency contact. Her mom had not shown up for work for over two weeks, did not answer her phone, and when a co-worker went to her home, no one answered the door.

LYDIA DROVE TO HER house. Her brown Oldsmobile Cutlass was in the driveway. She rang the doorbell and waited. She pounded on the door and yelled, "Mom, it's me." No answer. She saw shadows move inside. "Open up, I know that you're in there." She continued to pound on the door. "If you don't open this door right now, I am going to scream so loud that all the neighbors will hear and come rushing to your door," she threatened. "One, two." She heard multiple locks and chains unlatch. Lydia grabbed the doorknob and turned.

An old, unkempt woman stood before her. She had bald spots on her head and flaky skin lesions on her hands and arms. She kept on pulling on her hair to cover the lesions on her cheek.

"You've gained weight," she greeted her. Some things never changed.

"Your boss called me. He said you haven't been to work in two weeks."

"Oh, it's only been a few hours. As soon as I finish mopping the kitchen floor I'm going to leave for work."

"Mom, you need help."

"I'm fine."

Lydia held the door open and stepped inside.

"Now go, I'm busy I've got to finish the floors before I can leave for work." Sunny tried to close the door and push Lydia out. Lydia refused to budge.

"I'm not leaving."

It began to drizzle. Lydia closed the door.

HER MOM'S UNTREATED OBSESSIVE-COMPULSIVE disorder had finally caught up with her. She had been washing her hair three times a day. She had dermatitis on her hands from constant washing, which developed into skin lesions that she picked at. Her house cleaning routine held her hostage. Her disability counselor required she start exposure and response prevention therapy. The therapy involved gradually exposing the patient to a feared object or obsession, such as dirt, and teaching the patient healthy ways to deal with it.

Philip and Lydia drove her mom to her first session. Philip knew his wife's nerves were frazzled and wanted to drive her down to her mother's house. When her mom opened the door, she jumped back.

"Hi, Mrs. Kim," Philip said, entering the house.

She just stared at him.

"We're here to drive you to your appointment."

"I'm not going," her mom said.

"Mom, it's a condition of your employment," Lydia said. She grabbed her mother's purse. "Come on, we're gonna be late," she said.

Philip picked up Mom's white sweater and held it beside him like a matador's cape. She glared at Philip and then at Lydia like a trapped animal. Finally, the tired bull slid her arms into her sweater.

With medication and therapy, within a month she was going to her sessions by herself. She still didn't leave the house much, she felt safer inside.

SIX MONTHS LATER, PHILIP and Lydia dropped by her mom's to give her the news. Lydia rang the doorbell and stepped back, leaving Philip to take the first hit. Her mom always seemed to be better behaved when he was around. He knocked on the door. "Mom, open up, it's us," Lydia yelled. They heard movement inside and then five deadbolts unlocked. She was pale. The top button to her pants was undone.

"Didn't I teach you any manners? You're to call first before you barge into someone's house," she scolded. Her heat-seeking missile always had a way of finding her daughter.

"We have some good news to share with you," Philip said.

She reluctantly allowed them to come in and they sat down on her plastic covered couch. She had Jasper Computer retirement forms, booklets, calculators, and pens lined up on her glass coffee table. She skillfully arranged her papers into towering piles.

"I don't know what I'll do with all my free time once I retire," she said.

"You'll be busy with your grandchild," Lydia said.

Mom paused, her mood shifted.

"When are you due?" she asked, rubbing her daughter's belly.

"We're going to pick her up today," Lydia said.

"You don't feel that big," she said, reaching for her stomach again. Lydia grabbed her hand and swiped it away. "You should eat more," she said.

"Mom, I'm not pregnant," Lydia yelled.

"Stop working so much, and what kind of job is that anyway, listening to people complain about their problems all day? You absorb all their pain, not good for baby."

"Mom, I'm not pregnant," Lydia repeated.

"What?"

"We are adopting a Vietnamese girl, her parents–" Philip tried to explain.

"Why aren't you having your own?" she demanded.

"I told you she wouldn't understand," Lydia said to Philip.

"Her parents died and she–" he tried to continue.

"The purpose of a woman is to bear sons," she interrupted.

"Then you haven't served your purpose, have you?" Lydia slapped down a picture of Jamie on the table and stormed out.

Philip sat next to Sunny on the couch. They heard the horn honking and Lydia's rant of "Come on, let's go," coming from the driveway. Philip turned the picture over and handed it to Sunny.

She stared at the photo of Jamie with her hair in two braids. She gasped and turned to Philip.

"What's her name?"

"Jamie. She was named in honor of Lieutenant James."

ONE OF THE DANGERS OF being an immigrant to a new country was that you were time-capsuled in the year that you left. Lydia's mom's values were set in 1976 and she held on to these beliefs that were no longer practiced in Korea. People in Korea had grown, and had adopted new values, leaving her mom stuck. Lydia believed that a culture was dynamic; one must grow a tradition. It was like taking the same notes and melody of a familiar song and making it your own. Nothing stayed the same.

Lydia realized that all parents did the best they could with the knowledge they had. Once you became an adult, you were completely responsible for your own happiness. There was no one to blame. All she could do was try her best, just as any other parent had done. She wanted to teach Jamie how to learn, teach her how to make skillful choices for herself, teach her to fight for her rights when necessary.

She liked being introduced simply as Lydia. When they got married, Philip kept his last name and she kept hers. He could change his if he wanted. No one called her Mrs. Namura, however Philip had been called Mr. Kim on occasion. Their daughter's name was Jamie Tran Kim Namura. Now Lydia had a new name. When she volunteered at her school, the kids called her Jamie's mom.

All mothers have a name and her mother's was Sunny.

Chapter Eight
SUNNY

AFTER PHILIP'S MOM AND dad retired, they opened up Namura's Drive-In in Oakland. They served up the best plate lunches in town, local style. Tutu, Philip's Grandma, had fallen ill and the entire Namura clan went to Hawaii to support her. Philip took Jamie; Lydia stayed behind to hold down the fort. When she called her mother to help her at the Drive-In, Sunny hesitated. It had been almost a decade since Lydia had asked her mother for anything.

Sunny was pleased with herself for her commitment to therapy. She had shown dedication to her own healing and had been making excellent progress, according to her counselor. When she recognized her compulsion to repeat a task, she took three deep breaths and centered herself. She only mopped her floor once a week instead of three times a day, because she now was more self-aware. Maybe she just needed someone to talk to, someone who would not judge her behavior and tried to help her. She felt ready to reenter the world, even though she had been feeling bloated and her pants felt too tight. She chalked it up to middle age spread.

During the lunch rush, a distinguished Asian man came in. Everyone stopped to gawk when he entered. He was tall, grey haired, with a gentle Buddha face. He had presence. A calm followed him into the restaurant. He ordered a kalbi plate and then sat down. He was in his early sixties. Sunny was in the kitchen making sure the new batch of kalbi marinade was just right. She dipped her pinky into the bowl, and flicked her tongue against it. Satisfied, she laid the ribs in the marinade and then came out to the front. She suddenly stopped in her tracks and then ran back into the kitchen. She peeked from behind the curtain of the delivery window.

Minutes later, she reappeared. She had pulled off her hat, exposing her short salt and pepper hair that had grown back. She had put on lipstick. She checked herself once more in the stainless steel napkin holder and then marched straight to him.

"Hanjin, is that you?" she asked. The man studied her for a long time. He didn't say anything, just stared. His mind was flipping through a Rolodex trying to place her.

"Do I know you?" he asked.

Embarrassed, she said, "I'm sorry, I thought you were someone else." She turned to leave.

"Wait," he said and grabbed her arm. He regarded her with distain, his furrowed brow loosened, but then returned.

"I'm sorry, I made a mistake." She tried to step away but he tightened his grip. She winced in pain.

"For the past thirty-five years, not a day has gone by that I didn't remember what you did to me," he said. "That day, you changed who I am."

"I'm sorry," she said, shaking.

Lydia delivered his kalbi plate to him. He turned his gaze to her.

"Mom, are you ok?" she asked.

"This is my daughter, Lydia," she said. He let her go. He extended his hand and Lydia cautiously shook it while mining her mom for clues. He held her hand a little longer than was comfortable.

"It's nice to meet you, Lydia. I'm Hanjin," he said with a wide, beautiful smile. "She has your eyes, Sunny."

The kitchen needed Sunny so she apologized again and left.

Lydia returned to the counter, keeping a close eye on him. He first held his hands in prayer and bowed his head for a moment then he tore into his kalbi like a kid, licking his fingers and smacking his lips. She found Sunny soulfully watching him leave. This time he walked out of her life.

Sunny lowered herself into the chair where he had sat. It was still warm. His warmth seeped through her buttocks. He had eaten his kalbi ribs clean and neatly folded his napkin under his plate. She held his napkin to her lips. A faint smell of him remained. Under his plate, she found his business card. Hanjin Cho, Chairman of Dehan Computers.

GROWING UP, HER DAUGHTER never knew what Sunny was talking about when she would tell her the reason she couldn't buy her a new bicycle was the money had to go into her *hee-mong*, hope account. Lydia didn't find out about it until her dad lost it all in the stock market and Sunny filed for divorce. Sunny was furious that she had to start from scratch, again.

Ever since that day at the restaurant, Sunny could not stop talking about going to North Korea. Going to North Korea became her new obsession.

"Why can't you just go then?" Lydia asked, after hearing her talk about it for the past hour as they watched Jamie play at the park.

"It's complicated, they don't call it the hermit kingdom for nothing," Sunny said. They sat down on a wooden bench.

"Most things worthwhile are–complicated that is," Lydia said.

Sunny gave a long sigh and continued.

"At one point, well connected US citizens were allowed to go to North Korea as long as they had the money to make the bribes. But since 1994, when Kim Il Sung died and left his son, Kim Jong Il in power, it has become more difficult."

"Difficult or impossible?"

"The North Korean economy is in shambles and there is widespread famine. There are reports of millions of its citizens dying of starvation. Even if I figured out a way to get into North Korea, I would not be able to travel freely."

"So it is possible."

"Yes, the fortunate few. They met their relatives but they have to continue to send money. If the money stops, the family members are sent to work in the mines."

"Sorry, Mom, I didn't realize it was still that difficult to get into North Korea. I thought it was like crossing the border into Mexico or Canada," Lydia said.

"I have to find my sister, Nabi. I promised my father." Lydia put her arm around her mom's shoulders and gave her a squeeze. Jamie handed her grandma a picture she just drew.

"*Halmoni*, this one is you and this one is Mom," Jamie said as she pointed at the picture.

"What a beautiful job you did," Sunny said. "You are smart and gifted." She put Jamie on her lap and twirled the child's pigtails with her finger.

"*Halmoni, ppo ppo.*" Jamie gave Sunny a kiss.

Chapter Nine
HANJIN

HANJIN FLEW INTO SAN Jose from Seoul on his corporate jet to celebrate his *hwan-gap*, sixtieth birthday with his son. He couldn't believe that in five years they would be in the new millennium. In the olden days, living long enough for one complete zodiac cycle of sixty years was a rarity. He thanked God for protecting him; he could have perished a hundred times during the war. His son was now the CEO of Dehan Computers with subsidiaries in Silicon Valley. Since Hanjin's retirement, he served as the Chairman of the Board. He knew it was time for the next generation to take over. A wise man must realize that after a certain age, he is not going to be the smartest, strongest, or the most handsome man in the room. In order to cross over successfully into middle age and beyond, he must accept his new role of mentor, advisor, and helper, no longer needing to bask in the spotlight, no longer needing to prove himself.

He was tired, tired of battle, yet he easily recalled the hunger of being a young man. The fire in the belly, the desire to succeed, the desperate need for validation and approval. But now, like a wounded animal, he wanted to find a comfortable patch of leaves to lie in and rest. Yet, peace eluded him, he was haunted by unfinished business.

Every time Hanjin thought of his mother, he was filled with guilt and shame for not being able to live up to his responsibilities. Not because he didn't want to. Desire had nothing to do with it. Politics, power of wills, fate in the hands of strangers who play war upon others' land.

He left her in the darkness of night, black coal on his face, a skinny teenager with gawky long limbs. She packed him three rice balls, a handful of chestnuts, and dried pollack for the journey to his uncle's house. "Keep your head down, move quickly, but don't run. Don't bring any attention to yourself." She spoke rapidly with an urgent need to tell him everything. "You can come home in a week when the Communist recruiters have left our village," she instructed. She slipped off her gold wedding band and placed it inside his breast pocket. "If you get in trouble, use this. Go, now." Her eyes welled up. Hanjin rushed out into the courtyard, paused and turned to see her, a thin frail figure on the stoop. He closed the brass door behind him and headed toward the chestnut orchard. If he had known this was the last time he would see her, would he have said something? Would he have hugged her? Would he have held her hand against his cheek? What would he do differently if he had known it was the last time? With each passing year, his memories of her face faded.

Hanjin's childhood came to an abrupt halt as the world he once knew ceased to exist. The war forced him to become a man. There was no time to ponder his next move. Survival was his only goal. He escaped to Pusan along with eighty percent of the Korean population. He built an A-frame out of pieces of wood and carried loads for the UN soldiers. Because he was working all day, he wasn't able to regularly attend the makeshift school for refugee children and fell behind in his studies.

His determination to return to his mother fueled his everyday existence. In the middle of the war, an opportunity arose. He bribed merchants for a ride in their cargo truck. They were heading north to fortify the troops with supplies. Caught in a mob of refugees heading south, they were stuck. Fighter jets boomed overhead. They couldn't even get past the next city, Taegu.

In 1953, the war was declared over, but that wasn't the complete truth. The war resulted in essentially a stalemate and a ceasefire agreement dividing the country once again. No contact with the enemy was allowed.

Hanjin left Pusan and headed north riding on tops of boxcars along with hundreds of refugees. Wailing orphans and amputated veterans lay in the streets helpless among the crumbling buildings. He eventually found Mina, his *nuna* in Seoul. His older sister's wealthy politician husband had divorced her for not bearing him a son. She worked as a *gisaeng* to help pay for his schooling while he worked as a delivery boy for the American base. But his desire to return home to his mother was foremost on his mind.

Hanjin tried again. He boarded a bus heading north. Not more than an hour had passed when a South Korean soldier stopped the bus and ordered all the passengers to get off. Hanjin tried to pass a weathered sign that read, '38th Parallel: Beyond this point is North Korea'. His heart filled with anticipation that he could finally go home. The soldier stopped him with his rifle. "No one can go beyond this point," he said. "Anyone who steps into the next three miles will be shot."

Hanjin's hopes of returning home to North Korea were shattered. But that was not the event that made him the kind of man he became. The last time Hanjin saw Sunny's face was behind a wedding veil. He couldn't believe that she had gone through with it. He punched holes in the walls, pounded his fist on the hard *ondol* floor until they bled. None of it loosened the tightness he felt in his throat. Mina, his sister, found him delirious, mumbling to himself. Even strong minds crumbled under strain. She tried to soothe him, but it was of no use. "The best revenge is a life well lived," she said as she stroked his back. "You'll show them, you'll see."

His rage fueled his ambition. He worked furiously making deliveries to the US Army base, to corporations, and to government offices. His day started at four in the morning and ended after midnight. Between school and work, not a minute was left unprotected from thoughts of her.

A year later, Hanjin completed his engineering degree. As Seoul rose from the ashes, the siblings' lives began to improve bit by bit. They moved into a rental and purchased their first refrigerator. Hanjin started working at Dehan Electronics designing electrical circuit boards. He worked eighty-hour weeks and was rewarded with promotions, bonuses, and awards for his hard work and dedication to the company.

MEANWHILE, MINA WORKED IN a windowless sweatshop. In a dimly lit warehouse, over a hundred women sewed wigs on their machines. A young woman tried on a curly blonde wig and her male supervisor docked her a week's pay.

When Mina learned that the warehouse men were paid double the women's salary, she spoke to a secret group of twenty female co-workers. "We must force them to pay us our proper wages. The only way we can pressure them is by forming a union." The following week, she led a demonstration of fifty women to the Blue House. They carried banners and chanted.

"Equal pay for equal work," Mina roared.

"Equal pay for equal work," the women followed suit.

The men from the factory threw buckets of excrement on the women and beat them with clubs. The women scattered. A man poured a bucket of excrement over Mina's head. He howled with laughter. Mina wiped her face with her sleeve.

"Eat this and go home where you belong," he said.

"You bastard, you'll pay for this," she promised.

With the help of an attorney she knew from her former life as a *gisaeng*, she sued the factory. A year later, she became the first female supervisor. She instituted a mandatory ten-minute afternoon break where the women could try on any wig they liked and strike their best movie star poses. The energy in the warehouse shifted in an instant. Laughter filled the air.

BY THE EARLY SEVENTIES, Hanjin had been working at Dehan Electronics for five years when the CEO asked that he join him in his office. Hanjin entered and bowed.

"Come sit down, I have some exciting news." The CEO motioned to his leather couch. Hanjin was stunned by the breathtaking view of the city from the corner office.

"Your commitment to my company has been admirable, I am very impressed with your work."

"Thank you, sir."

"As you know, we are expanding at a rapid pace and we need to conquer new markets. With your excellent English, I want you to head up our marketing efforts in the United States."

"Thank you, you will not be disappointed," Hanjin said and bowed.

"Congratulations, Mr. Vice President." The CEO shook his hand and patted him on the back. Hanjin turned to leave.

"And one more thing, there is someone I'd like you to meet tomorrow," he said.

HANJIN WAITED AT A café for the CEO and his daughter. When they arrived, the three of them sat at the same table. She was in her early-thirties, plain and frail. Her mother had recently passed away. She was so pale she looked like she had just seen a ghost.

MINA FIXED HANJIN'S BOW tie and then brushed the sleeve of his tuxedo.

"I wish mother could see you on your wedding day," Mina sighed. Then she held his face in her hands and asked, "You've only known her for a month. Are you sure?"

"He's been like a father to me," he answered.

A CROWD OF REPORTERS gathered in front of the Blue House. Mina, dressed in a smart, blue business suit, confidently approached them.

"Is it true you intend to run for Congress?" a female reporter asked.

"It's about time, it is 1972," Mina declared.

"If elected, you'll become South Korea's first congresswoman. What do you think your chances are?"

"Korean women are fed up being treated like second class citizens. It's time for our voices to be heard!" Thousands of women cheered with enthusiasm. "Let our voices erupt releasing centuries of suppressed anger, disappointment, and unfulfilled expectations. Our father, husband or son will no longer define us. We will define ourselves."

HANJIN BELIEVED PEOPLE WERE either a success or a failure; there was no middle ground. When he became a success, he showed it. His house was a towering two-story colonial designed after Tara from 'Gone with the Wind'. He sat with his wife and his father-in-law in his Queen Anne inspired living room.

"I remember going to the United States for the first time to attend Stanford. I was so scared; I carried my Korean English dictionary with me everywhere," his father-in-law said.

"It must have been tough," Hanjin said.

"It got easier with time," he said.

"I will first be meeting with computer firms in Silicon Valley."

"That's a sound strategy."

Hanjin's wife brought in their baby and handed him to his grandfather.

"Oh, here's my precious grandson," he said.

The baby boy bounced on his grandfather's knee and they both laughed with delight. When their eyes met, Hanjin smiled at his wife.

Chapter Ten
SUNNY

A S SUNNY GAZED OUT her plane window, she welcomed with recognition the sights below–the mountains, rivers, and the four gates surrounding the city–Seoul. It had been over twenty years since Sunny left Korea. She had watched the 1988 Seoul Olympics on TV and witnessed how modernized it had become. Upon landing in Seoul ten years later, her first step onto Korean soil felt familiar yet new. She had returned purposeful.

First, she went to her parents' grave. The leaves on the trees were blood red. She climbed to the mountaintop where a large grass covered mound stood and placed white mums at the grave. Next, she placed rice, fish cakes, and *soju* in front of the grave and bowed three times. The north beckoned her.

The next day, Sunny strode into the Reunification Center and asked for Director Cho. Moments later, Hanjin appeared. They bowed to each other, and then awkwardly shook hands and sat down in his office.

"Thanks for seeing me," Sunny said.

"Actually, I was surprised to hear from you," Hanjin said.

"I'm hoping you can point me in the right direction."

"We'll try our best."

"Thank you. How often do you work here?"

"My wife passed away five years ago and there is only so much golf I can play," he replied.

Sunny felt joy bursting up. She lowered her head and bit her lip to try to suppress her smile.

"I'm sorry for your loss."

"Thank you." They sat in silence. Hanjin leaned back in his chair, his elbow supported by his hand; he drummed his temple with his index and middle fingers. He swallowed.

"Is your husband here with you?"

He cares, he still cares, Sunny rejoiced. She couldn't hold it in anymore.

"No, I've been divorced for over ten years," she blurted out too enthusiastically. She covered her mouth and blushed.

Trying to recover from her embarrassment, she changed the topic to the task at hand.

"Can you help me find my sister, Nabi?"

"Fill out this form detailing how you lost her and how old she would be now. Do you have a picture of her?" he asked, handing her the paperwork.

Sunny handed Hanjin the picture. Their hands brushed lightly, and her face began to twitch.

"This is my only picture of my family."

In the photo, Youngho and Sunny stood in the back while Uma and Apa sat in the front with Nabi on Apa's knee.

"Getting our picture taken was such serious business then," he said.

"No one dared crack a smile," Sunny said, beaming.

He scanned the photo and gave it back to her. A database was being built so that reunification of lost families could be made quickly once both sides reached an agreement.

"You're not alone. There are over a million members of separated families in South and North Korea."

THE NEXT DAY, SUNNY returned to the Reunification Center.

"Have you heard from your North Korean source?" she asked.

Hanjin shook his head and then smiled. "Just because you decided this was the time to start your search, it doesn't mean everyone else has been just sitting idle waiting for you."

"I'm just eager to get going."

"I understand your impatience."

"What can I do in the meantime?"

"Tomorrow I'm going to the Military Research Institute for Defense to do research on war orphans. Do you want to come along?"

HANJIN PICKED HER UP in his black Jaguar. Their day started at the Statue of Brothers, two soldiers on a cracked hemispherical pedestal. The plaque read: 'Based on a dramatic true story of two brothers who met each other on the battlefield, this statue symbolizes brotherly love transcending ideology'.

The day floated by as if she were in a dream. They first pored over manuscripts at the Research Institute. They had lunch at Diamond Mountain restaurant where Hanjin picked up the tenderest part of the fish's belly with his chopsticks and placed it in her rice bowl. They climbed up to Namsan Tower and marveled at the city below. They meandered through the Secret Garden in Ch'angdokkung Palace where lotus flowers blossomed on muddy ponds. Under bright, colorful pavilions with intricate wall decor, they wistfully watched a young couple in their wedding attire being photographed in front of the garden. Hanjin bought Sunny a red bean bun from Kyro Bakery. Finally, they stood in front of a computer store.

"Are you sure this is where father's bookstore used to stand?" Sunny asked.

Hanjin turned the map around. The street now had high rises on both sides.

"Memory is an unreliable historian," Hanjin said.

"I barely recognize these streets," Sunny said. All those years she tried so hard to suppress her memories of Seoul, yet now that she was back, she didn't know what really existed and what she had fabricated in her mind.

Six years before, when the LA riots broke out, she watched bloody Korean storeowners defending their stores. Her thoughts brought her back to when she found a bloodied Hanjin lying in these very streets during the student riots over three decades ago. She may not have remembered the exact details of the event, but the devastation she felt was real. She was tired of fighting the past. Her past refused to stay buried and now she boldly welcomed back all the shattered pieces of herself that she had denied ever existed. She no longer had to fake wholeness.

The following week, they went to the Blue House to see Honorable Congresswoman Mina Cho. Mina, now in her late sixties, wore her long, white hair loose. Beneath well-earned survival lines on her face, her inner beauty shined even brighter, more powerful. She pumped Sunny's hand and then smiled.

"Please sit," she said.

"This is Sunny," Hanjin said.

"I know. It's been a long time," Mina said.

"How are you?" Sunny asked.

"Fun and games with the big boys."

"Ever since Mina got elected to office, the men have had to change their ways," Hanjin said.

"I outrank most of them in seniority, that doesn't make me very popular, especially with my ex-husband." Mina roared a loud belly laugh and winked at Sunny.

"Revenge sure is sweet," Mina said.

"How are the negotiations with North Korea coming along?" Hanjin asked.

"Damn slow. It's ironic how we can't seem to talk to each other without having to throw a God damn tea party with the Chinese and the Americans," she said.

"Do you think Korea will ever be reunified?" Sunny asked.

Mina pondered her response. "Discontent cascades like a house of cards." Her fingers met like a teepee and then she slammed her palms down on her desk. "Countries where people routinely hide their true opinions are prone to sudden, explosive political mobilization. Only time will tell."

"We haven't had much luck finding my sister," Sunny said.

"Stay tough, don't give up," Mina advised and pumped her fist in the air.

ANOTHER WEEK HAD PASSED and Sunny felt anxious. She just wanted to know what happened to Nabi. Was she still alive? If not, when did she die? She needed to know. She sat in her hotel room watching TV, waiting for Hanjin's call. The newscaster recounted how three months ago, five hundred cows boarded Hyundai trucks. The trucks passed through into North Korea on Reunification Bridge. Hyundai Group founder, Chung Ju-Yang, brought the cows to North Korea in exchange for a discussion of a tourism project at Diamond Mountain, North Korea.

Up next, the Reunification show. "Welcome to the reunion show. Please tell us the circumstances surrounding how you lost your sister," the host asked.

"Our house was bombed in Seoul and both of our parents died. We were starving and an old woman gave us some food. The train stopped in Taegu and we got off to go to the bathroom. The crowds were pushing to get back on to the top of the boxcars. We got up there and as the train was leaving, my sister fell off. I screamed for the train to stop, but it kept on going. I haven't been able to find her since," the woman said.

"If there is anyone out there watching named Lee Bok Sum, date of birth June 24, 1947, who lost her sister under these circumstances, please call us immediately," the host urged. "Last week, we got a call from this gentleman's sister. Today, in our studios, they will be reunited for the first time in over forty years." Sunny blew her nose, and wiped her tear-streaked face. Then the phone rang.

HANJIN HANDED SUNNY A computer printout. "Her name is Kim Nabi. Her birthday is January 20, 1947."

"No, Nabi's birthday is January 20, 1942. Besides this woman could be old enough to be our mother." Sunny slumped in her chair.

"Their suffering hides their true age. The adults seem much older than they actually are and the children much younger, due to malnutrition. I'm sorry to have raised your hopes up," Hanjin said.

"It's been almost a month," Sunny pleaded.

"I haven't heard from my North Korean contact yet," he said.

Suddenly, a searing pain shot through Sunny's abdomen. She grabbed her stomach and collapsed onto the floor.

INSIDE THE HOSPITAL ROOM, Hanjin helped Sunny sit up in bed. "You heard the doctor, he recommended you return to the US for more tests."

"I just fainted, that's all. It must be something I ate." Hanjin's concern spread across his face.

AT KIMPO AIRPORT, SUNNY waited to board the plane. She felt weak and defeated. They announced her seat number for boarding. She picked up her carry-on and reluctantly headed for the gate.

"Sunny, stop," Hanjin screamed, running towards her. "Sunny, Nabi is alive. I received verification from my North Korean counterpart."

"You found her?"

"Yes, and the first tourist cruise to Diamond Mountain, North Korea, is scheduled to leave in a few days."

Hanjin squeezed her hand.

WHEN SUNNY RETURNED TO her hotel, she called her daughter. Lydia and Jamie were having breakfast.

"Mom, did your flight get in early?"

"No, Lydia, I'm still in Seoul."

"You said your doctor ordered you to come home."

"I'm going to North Korea, they found Nabi."

Jamie made flower designs on the table with her soggy Fruit Loops.

"Stop that!" Lydia scolded.

"I've got to go," Sunny said.

"Mom, you're in no condition to go traipsing through North Korea."

"I won't be alone, Hanjin–."

"–You barely know him. Come home now," Lydia insisted.

"Lydia, listen to me."

"Get on the next plane," Lydia ordered.

"Lydia, I am proud of you. You're a good wife, mother, and daughter."

"Mom, stop talking like this."

"Just remember who you are."

"Mom–."

Sunny hung up the phone.

HANJIN AND SUNNY WERE among eight hundred tourists gathered below deck on the Diamond Mountain cruise ship. The North Korean tour guide began to sing '*Arirang*', a Korean folk song. The tourists joined in.

"Do not engage in any conversation or photograph any North Koreans. There are dire consequences for disobeying the rules. Please do not wear sunglasses while you are in North Korea. Only high-ranking government officials are allowed to wear them," the tour guide warned. At Changjon Port, they exited the ship.

"Our first step back on North Korean land," Hanjin said.

"The same but different," Sunny replied.

They filed onto buses. A large political slogan read, 'Let's protect life with revolutionary headquarters led by Comrade Kim Jong Il'. The bus passed sun scorched, emaciated men and women along the road carrying heavy bags on their heads and backs. They saw shabby farmers who used only simple tools such as shovels, picks, and handcarts. No one appeared to pay any attention to the bus or its occupants.

Hanjin and Sunny climbed Kumgangsan, Diamond Mountain. They recalled old Korean folk songs that reminded them that they couldn't die before seeing Kumgangsan. The craggy peaks and dramatic waterfalls were truly breathtaking; the fall colors sparkled as a cool breeze rustled the leaves. The majestic mountain deserved its prize as the most revered landscape described in Korean fables and songs. They came to a huge boulder carved with the slogan, 'Kim Jong Il the lodestar of self-reliance'. The tour guide explained that more than six hundred dynamite sticks were needed to carve one eight letter slogan. The carving produced 370 truckloads of rock fragments.

When they reached the top of the mountain, Hanjin set an offering of dried fish, rice and soju for his parents upon a large rock. He bowed three times. With tear-filled eyes, Hanjin turned to Sunny, "Mother would be over a hundred years old if she were still alive. I haven't been a good son. I haven't been able to take care of her like I promised my father in this life or the afterlife." Sunny and Hanjin embraced for the first time in thirty-five years, tears streamed down her face. Hanjin wiped his tears and gazed into Sunny's eyes and gave her a soft, tender kiss. They embraced as one on top of Diamond Mountain.

MUSIC BEGAN IN THE Kim Il Sung musical hall. A musical dance production in tribute to the great leader was under way. The valiant twenty-something Kim Il Sung, dressed in green fatigues, fought off the evil Japanese. In the audience, Sunny and Hanjin shifted in their seats. Sunny's hands trembled and when Hanjin went to grab them, she folded her hands in her lap. She knew the risk involved. Just when there was hope that she could be finally happy with her true love. Yet she couldn't turn back. She had come too far. She had to see this through. She squeezed his hand and let go, but he held on. She laid his hand in his lap. She tore herself from his pleading eyes and excused herself.

A BATHROOM ATTENDANT MOPPED the floor. Sunny washed her hands, entered the first stall, flushed three times, returned to the sink and washed her hands again. When she looked up into the mirror, her eyes met the attendant's. The bathroom attendant took off her scarf and handed it to Sunny.

In the rear of the building, dressed as a bathroom attendant, Sunny nervously scanned the empty parking lot. She paced back and forth. She placed her hand below her ribcage and deliberately slowed her inhalations and exhalations. She could hear the musical numbers coming from the auditorium. Kim Il Sung fought off the evil capitalist with the help of his courageous Chinese comrades. Her thoughts returned to Hanjin nervously twisting his program. She waited anxiously.

On stage, the people of North Korea celebrated their victory in the Korean War, waving a large red flag. The dancers raised Kim Il Sung on their shoulders. Music ended. Applause filled the hall.

Sunny turned around and started to go back into the building. Just then a black sedan with a Pyongyang license plate pulled up. The rear passenger window went down. A lavishly dressed woman in her fifties appeared. She slowly took off her sunglasses.

"Nabi, is that you?" Sunny asked and then she was pulled into the car.

Seated next to her, Sunny held her younger sister's face in her hands and hugged her. Nabi's mascara smeared down her face. They cried and laughed at the same time.

"Uma and Apa?" Nabi asked.

"They passed away years ago. How did you–"

"–I told the communist soldiers that I was an orphan and that my family died in the war. A childless couple raised me as their own. I became a dancer in the musicals and married a decorated war hero."

"How did you know?"

"I bribed many people to see you today. But don't try to contact me again or my family's lives will be in danger." Nabi handed Sunny a weathered, folded red cloth embroidered with swans.

In the front parking lot, Hanjin headed towards the bus with the other tourists. He nervously glanced around.

Sunny finally let go of her sister's hand through the window of the sedan as it pulled away.

The tourists filed onto the bus. A guard spoke into his walkie-talkie. The seat next to Hanjin was empty.

Sunny heard the North Korean soldiers stomp down the hall with their rifles. The soldiers rushed into the empty bathroom. A Korean soldier opened the door of the first stall with his rifle. The stall was empty. The second stall, empty. The third, empty.

Sunny stepped out of the last stall in her own clothes. The older soldier pointed his rifle in her face. The eager soldier grabbed her arm and led her out of the bathroom.

THE INTERROGATION ROOM WAS bare except for a long table and two chairs.

"Take her passport."

"Yes, lieutenant." The older soldier took Sunny's passport and left. Another guarded the door.

"What were you doing in the rear parking lot?" the youthful lieutenant demanded.

"What are you talking about?" Sunny said.

"Who was in the black sedan?"

"What sedan?" she replied.

"Answer me."

The lieutenant slapped her. She stood up out of the chair. "You can't keep me here, I'm a US citizen."

"We'll do as we like," he sneered. "Captain Park will deal with you." He pushed her back down into the chair.

A distinguished elderly man entered the room. His walnut uniform sparkled with stars and medals on his broad chest. The soldiers saluted him.

"Captain Park, this is the missing woman from the tourist cruise," the lieutenant explained.

"Leave us." He stared intently at Sunny. She matched his gaze. He sat down across from her. They glared at each other in silence.

"Why are you here?" he asked.

"I'm a US citizen, you have to let me go."

"Where do you live in the US?"

"California."

"What are you doing in Korea?"

"Vacation."

"How's the tour?"

"I've seen what I came to see."

He scribbled on a piece of paper, folded it and pushed it across the table. Sunny unfolded the piece of paper and raised her head.

"Please tell my sister in Seoul that I'm alive."

She nodded.

The Captain called his men back.

"Lieutenant, escort this woman back to the bus."

"But sir, she broached a restricted military area," the Lieutenant argued.

"Lieutenant, that will be all," Captain Park roared.

The Lieutenant led Sunny back to the parking lot where the bus awaited its final passenger.

"Get on your knees," he said as he pushed Sunny down on the cement parking lot. He laid his heavy boot into her back. "You think you can just get away that easily?"

Sunny heard a gun cock. When she turned her head, she saw terror on Hanjin's face plastered against the locked door of the bus.

"You are a traitor." He threw her passport on her head. "A citizen of our mortal enemy."

She took a deep breath.

LANIKAI BEACH, LOCATED ON the windward side of the island of Oahu with its mile long stretch of fine grain sand, sparkling turquoise green waters protected by a wide off shore reef was postcard perfect. Flanked by twin islands Mokumanu and Mokulua, now bird sanctuaries, Lanikai Beach lived up to its Hawaiian name "Heavenly Sea." A small group gathered as the sun hovered over the horizon.

The whiff of pikake leis astounded the senses as the waves gently rolled in and out. For centuries, the Mokuluas had witnessed beginnings and endings. For Sunny, this wasn't a beginning but a continuation of a story that began with an offer of an azuki bean bun almost four decades ago on the streets of Seoul.

Her groom wore a white linen shirt with rolled up white slacks. A maile lei, bestowing honor and respect, hung from his neck in an open-ended horseshoe fashion. She wore an ivory dress with capped sleeves and a matching maile lei around her neck. Her hair was pulled back and adorned with purple orchids. She wiggled her toes in the soft sand. The evening breeze blew wisps of her hair onto her face. Hanjin gently tucked her hair behind her ear. The minister blew the conch shell signaling the beginning of the ceremony. She asked the spirits to witness and bless this union of two people choosing to spend the rest of their lives together, promising to help each other become the best they can be as they head towards the last chapters of their lives together, that they may uplift each other and recognize the inner light within them. Sunny faced Hanjin and they tied the loose ends of each maile lei together to form a circle enclosing them. Next, they leaned in, touched foreheads and exchanged "ha"–the breath of life. Sunny knew she would never be separated from her love again.

AFTER SEVERAL CHANGES OF ownership, the Ala Moana Hotel was showing its age. No matter how many facelifts and remodels it had, the fact that it was aging was undeniable. When the hotel opened its doors in 1970, it was the tallest building in Hawaii at thirty-six stories high. Located at the gateway to Waikiki, during its heyday, many notable celebrities such as Muhammad Ali and Jack Lord of *Hawaii 5-0* stayed there. The suite had a faint scent of cigarettes, and under the chair leg there was a stubborn red wine stain. The tub had new grout. But no amount of cleaning was going to bring it back to its original luster. Yet, its usefulness remained. It had provided a brief sanctuary to weary travelers.

Hanjin had stayed at the Ala Moana Hotel during his stopovers in Honolulu when he flew between Seoul and California. Many finer, newer hotels had been built since then, but he felt nostalgic and wanted to stay at the Ala Moana.

THEIR RECEPTION WAS HELD on the penthouse floor overlooking the skyline of Honolulu. Sunny and Hanjin's dinner was interrupted several times by the sound of clinking glasses signaling them to kiss. They obliged their guests with pleasure from a shy kiss on her cheek at first to a full passionate kiss toward the last course.

For the first dance, Kimo, Philip's cousin, strummed his ukulele and played 'What a Wonderful World'. Hanjin took Sunny's hand and led her to the dance floor. He placed her right hand on top of his. When he pushed forward with his upper body, she pushed back, building a strong frame.

As Kimo crooned, Sunny confidently looked into Hanjin's eyes, assured in her dance steps. She couldn't help herself from smiling widely with all her teeth showing.

Lydia and Philip had joined the bride and groom on the dance floor. Sunny smiled and let go of Hanjin's hand. She tapped Lydia on her shoulder and cut in, taking Philip's hand. Philip was taken aback at first, but soon, they moved to a comfortable groove.

Sunny returned Philip to Lydia and Jamie dancing. Next, Sunny danced with Jamie. She lifted her arm and Jamie twirled, finishing with a bow. She kissed her grandma on her cheek. Sunny sashayed into her awaiting knight's arms.

"For the bride," Lydia said with a mischievous grin as she handed Sunny a gift bag with yellow plumerias. Sunny peered into the bag and grabbed something then dropped it back into the bag. She removed a small blue *bojagi*. She untied the knots revealing a chestnut and date, Korean traditional gifts given to the bride from her in-laws with the wish for many children.

Sunny squeezed the chestnut and date in her palm and hugged Lydia.

"Have fun," Lydia whispered in her mom's ear.

After thanking their guests, Sunny and Hanjin headed down to their suite.

HANJIN CARRIED HER OVER the threshold.

While Sunny went into the bathroom to change, Hanjin undressed and pulled on his blue pinstriped pajamas. He propped up his pillow and hopped onto the bed. She came out in her pink, long-sleeved, nightgown. Her face was freshly cleaned with a gleam of moisturizer. He smiled and lifted the covers. She joined him and rested her head on his chest. She inhaled his scent. His arms around her, she did not feel trapped but comforted.

The next morning, she awoke and found him next to her. She wondered if she was in a dream. Was she really married to him? She touched his hand to make sure he was real. His once calloused hands were now soft with brown age spots. She stroked his face, his cheek, and felt the prick of his grey whiskers. She ran her fingers through his hair, down his neck, delighting in the texture of his skin. His eyes were still closed. She placed a light kiss on his lips, a sweet, quick peck. He opened his eyes, traced her lips with his fingers and held her cheek as he gave her a slow, savored kiss. She charged in with a passionate, hungry, wet kiss, exploring his tongue with hers. They continued their dance of discovery, savoring each new delight.

He pulled off his pajamas and she slipped off her nightgown. She pulled the covers over them. He rubbed his hand down her legs, calves, feet, and toes. She giggled and kicked his hand away. He spooned her from behind. They basked in the warmth and texture of each other's skin. When she felt him against her tailbone, she turned her head towards him and admitted that she hadn't done this in a long time.

"I haven't either," he responded. They smiled and then laughed at how awkward they felt. They were on a new adventure, approaching with beginners' minds. He kissed her neck and she gasped. He abruptly stopped, and asked if she was okay. She nodded. He kissed her chest, her stomach and tickled her side with the top of his head making her giggle. She caught her breath entangled in his arms. He peeked under the covers at her hot pink lacy panties. She asked him to wait, leaned over to the nightstand and pulled out a tube. He squeezed some on his fingertips and flicked it on her nose. "Here?" he asked. He then rubbed some on her nipples and drew circles around them with his finger. He kissed her fully and gently rubbed his lubricated fingers between the crease of her thighs and up over her clitoris and back down again. With the increasing pressure of each stroke, she shuddered.

His penis reached up to meet her hand. She rubbed her lubricated palm along the shaft in long strokes. She paused, encircled the head, and then returned to the shaft with greater force. He rolled on top of her with his weight on his elbows. His cardiologist had given him the green light. His heart had mended. When she felt him inside her, she grabbed his buttocks and pulled him deeper. Their bodies dissolved into the gap between breaths.

Their chests rose and fell in unison as they snuggled in each other's arms. She was safe.

She inhaled peace.

Chapter Eleven
LYDIA

THE SETTING SUN ILLUMINATED the majestic mountains surrounding their new home. Lydia had a private therapy practice and saw clients in her home office, formerly the garage. In Hawaiian, 'ohana' was the name given to the extra room off the main house. 'Ohana' also meant family and she felt privileged to be able to help her clients in her own home. Working at home gave her more time to be alone and re-energize. She loved being able to welcome her knight back home into their castle after a hard day of fighting dragons at the office. It also gave her more time to be with her daughter, Jamie, when she came home from school.

Lydia swirled the brush in a jar of grey water, squeezed the water out and handed the brush to Jamie. Jamie brushed the tip against the black ink stone and painted one last stroke on their bamboo tree. Lydia put her arms around

Jamie's shoulders as they proudly admired their work. Just then, Jamie broke her mom's embrace and ran into her bedroom. "I'll be right back."

Lydia's eyes were drawn to the photos on her desk. A photo of Mom with her parents, brother, and sister, a photo of Mom and Dad holding her as a baby, a photo of Philip and her in college, and a photo of Mom and Hanjin taken on their wedding day in Hawaii.

"Mom, look." Jamie handed Lydia her latest computer design: green rice plants in neat rows, figures in cone shaped hats hunched over in ankle deep brown water.

"That's terrific, Jamie. How'd you get the idea for your latest painting?"

"I don't know, I just paint."

LYDIA STARED INTO THE DMZ where her grandmother died, desperate to return home to North Korea to find her daughter, Nabi. The South Korean government had set up a cemetery in Im Jing Kang overlooking the river into North Korea, former North Koreans who wanted to be buried as close to North Korea as possible were buried there. These three miles had kept enemies apart for over fifty-five years. The enemies were of the same blood, same family.

Peering through the barbed wired fence at the DMZ, Lydia knew that she was the woman she was today because of, and in spite of, her mother.

The last time Lydia saw her mother, she was struck by the realization that she had never seen her so beautiful. As cancer spread from Sunny's ovaries throughout her body, she became weaker in body, but more radiant in spirit.

"Uma, I'm sorry," Lydia said and gave her mom a kiss on her forehead. Sunny shook her head.

"When you let go," Sunny said, "of judgment and expectations. . ." Lydia held Sunny's hand. Her dry, silky, palm was translucent.

"There's nothing to forgive."

"Uma," Lydia cried holding Sunny's palm against her cheek.

"Lydia, *saranghe.*

"I love you too, Mom."

She died in her sleep in her husband's arms nine months after their wedding.

LYDIA UNTIED THE ARMS of the royal blue *bojagi* embracing the urn. She opened the lid and scattered Sunny's ashes into no man's land.

She recited her favorite poem by Rumi, a Persian Muslim poet, to her mom.

"Out beyond the ideas of wrong doing and right doing there is a field . . . I'll meet you there. Where the soul lies down in that grass, the world is too full to talk about. Ideas, language, even the phrase 'each other' doesn't make any sense."

The once close to extinction red-crowned crane with its red hat, black gloves and white coat stood on one leg and then the other. His partner joined him in the dance.

LYDIA STOOD IN THE middle of her bright and airy kitchen. The vertical blinds danced in the breeze, clicking and clacking to the beat. She swirled the grains of rice in the pot and rinsed three times.

Jamie, in her plaid skirt and white shirt, announced her arrival by dropping her backpack on the kitchen floor.

"How was school?" Lydia asked.

"Mom, why aren't you using the rice cooker?"

"The fuse blew." Lydia added water into the pot with the rinsed rice. She poured the water out. She placed her hand in the pot on top of the rice and added water until it reached her knuckles. "I think this is how Mom knew how much water to pour in, I'm not sure." She dumped the water out again and started over.

"Can I help?" Jamie asked as she climbed on the barstool.

"Sure."

Jamie poked her index finger into the pot of rice. "The water should hit here," she said, pointing to the second joint of her finger.

Lydia placed her index finger in the rice next to Jamie's.

A PLASTIC TABLECLOTH WITH red anthuriums covered the teak picnic table. Silver chopsticks and a spoon with royal blue Chinese lettering sat next to the paper plates. A violet cymbidium orchid planted in bark and cork took center stage. Cucumber *kim chee*, jellyfish salad, lomi salmon, inari sushi, Vietnamese summer rolls and haupia pudding shared the table with jellied cranberry sauce, mashed potatoes and, of course, turkey.

Jamie made a moat in the middle of her mashed potato fortress and filled it with gravy. Hanjin placed his hand on the empty chair next to him. Lydia poured another glass of POG, passion orange guava juice, and handed it to him.

"Lydia, the stuffing is the best I've had," Hanjin said, helping himself to another scoop. "What's the secret?"

"I chopped the chestnuts so you can taste it in every bite."

Philip held two Pringles potato chips in his mouth and pecked his wife's neck with his beak. Lydia laughed and hugged her bird crusader. She was surrounded by love–and love is thicker than blood.

Postscript

THE KOREAN WAR RESULTED in 4.4 million casualties, including 2.5 million North and South Korean civilians, 1.9 million North and South Korean servicemen, 170,000 UN servicemen including 148,000 U.S. servicemen, 100,000 war orphans, and 1 million separated families.

To this day, the DMZ (Demilitarized Zone) separates North Korea and South Korea at the 38th parallel. The two countries never signed a peace treaty and are still technically at war. There is no contact allowed between citizens of North Korea and South Korea.

The 2.5-mile-wide no man's land that separates North and South Korea has become an unintended nature preserve where the red-crowned cranes, one of the rarest birds in the world, find sanctuary.

Acknowledgements

M Y CHILDHOOD MEMORIES DON'T include tales from the old country. My parents didn't talk about the past. Growing up, I felt a gap between us that could have been attributed to the typical teenage struggle for independence. Our misunderstandings, generational and cultural, were compounded by the nuance of language lost in translation as my parents commanded me in Korean and I talked back in English. As they grew older, memories of the past bubbled to the surface. Perhaps they were trying to protect me, for there is safety in not knowing. Perhaps time had given them the courage to heal. Perhaps I was finally ready to listen.

Textbooks in school didn't teach me much about the Korean War. The neglected middle child caught between WWII and Vietnam, it now demands to be remembered as part of America's history.

Firstly, I would like to thank my parents for sharing their stories with me. I am eternally grateful for their foresight to journey to this country and to raise me as a proud American woman of Korean descent, freest in the world. Thank you also to my siblings, James Park and Helen Park.

I am deeply grateful to the brave Korean War Veterans who risked their lives to save others. Without their sacrifice, I would not be here today.

Mahalo to all my friends and beta readers who read early drafts and offered thoughts: Jan Bovard, Robin Scanlon, Philippe Hema, Coral Mack, Pat Ishram, David Littlejohn, Janet Motooka, YeBong Park, Vicki Stoddard, Christine Osterwalder, Jen Aly, Barb Bosz, Susie Jenkins, Leilani Clark, Renee Newman, Shirley Matthews, Leslie Koziol, Catherine Robbins, Rebecca Hallford, Sheila Hufstetler, Catherine Tarleton, Gloria Blum, Barry Blum, and Dawn Henry.

Special thanks to my fellow Toastmasters, Andrea Pro, Lynn Bell, Mary Ellen Legay, and Charles Perez for their encouragement and support. My love and thanks to my fellow daughters of war, Marlene Shigekawa, S. Casper Wong, and Deborah Oakley Melvin.

Mahalo to Brandon W. Jones and Irwin Tang for their feedback and encouragement. Thanks to Debra Baumert, Rev. Deborah Knowles, and Rev. Jiko Nakade for spiritual and life counsel.

Thank you to my editor, Ken Darrow, for helping me polish this work. I apologize to all who have read and given feedback on various drafts that I have failed to mention. Thank you for your support and forgiveness.

I would not have been able to share this novel with the world without the love, support, kindness, humor, encouragement, and patience of my high school sweetheart, Keith Olson. Thank you for believing in me. I am honored to be travelling on this life journey with you and our four-legged companions who remind us that every day is a joyous event.

About the Author

MARY J. PARK is the winner of the 2009 Hawaii Writers Conference (formally Maui Writers Conference) Prose Writing Competition, an alumna of Squaw Valley Community of Writers and a Finalist for the Sundance Screenwriters Lab. Her poetry has been published in *Women's Voices of the 21st Century: Experiences that Shape Women*. A graduate of Smith College with a Master's in psychology, she lives on the Big Island of Hawaii with her high school sweetheart, a pair of Hungarian Vizslas and a pair of orange cream felines.

Made in the USA
Middletown, DE
27 April 2015